A DANGEROUS CHARADE

"Mama is in high alt. Indeed, I quite think she has forgotten the bargain we made," Diana said. There was a pause as she looked down at her feet and bit her lower lip with her pearl white teeth. "Sometimes I find myself forgetting this is not real," she confessed.

Stephen's heart quickened, and he squeezed her hand in his. This was the opportunity he had been seeking. "About that—" he began.

He felt a tap on his shoulder, and he turned and then stopped still in frozen horror. Diana stepped on his foot, and then clutched his arm to right herself at the sudden stop.

A part of him noticed that around them heads were turning, and the other couples were gradually coming to a halt as the inanely cheerful music continued on. But the rest of his attention was fixed on the man who stood before him.

"Dear brother, Miss Somerville," George said with a mocking gleam in his eye. "Forgive my tardiness, but I had to come and offer my congratulations."

"George," Stephen said. He could think of nothing else to say. He was all too conscious of Miss Somerville, who was trembling with fury by his side. . . .

BOOK YOUR PLACE ON OUR WEBSITE AND MAKE THE READING CONNECTION!

We've created a customized website just for our very special readers, where you can get the inside scoop on everything that's going on with Zebra, Pinnacle and Kensington books.

When you come online, you'll have the exciting opportunity to:

- View covers of upcoming books
- Read sample chapters
- Learn about our future publishing schedule (listed by publication month *and author*)
- Find out when your favorite authors will be visiting a city near you
- Search for and order backlist books from our online catalog
- Check out author bios and background information
- Send e-mail to your favorite authors
- Meet the Kensington staff online
- Join us in weekly chats with authors, readers and other guests
- Get writing guidelines
- AND MUCH MORE!

**Visit our website at
http://www.kensingtonbooks.com**

THE WRONG
MR. WRIGHT

Patricia Bray

ZEBRA BOOKS
Kensington Publishing Corp.
http://www.kensingtonbooks.com

One

If one were to stroll down St. James Street, past the fashionable shops and well-known clubs, eventually one would come to an unremarkable red-brick building. The ground floor was occupied by a bookseller, whose merchandise often spilled out of the store onto trestle tables which partially blocked the sidewalk. If one were to walk past the overflowing tables and turn into the small alley on the left-hand side of the building, he would find a plain wooden door with a brass knocker. There was no sign on the door, since none was needed. Those personages who ventured this far knew that this door was the entrance to the Explorers' Society, one of the least known and most select of London's Gentlemen's clubs.

The Explorers' Society occupied the top three stories of the building. As clubs went, it was unremarkable. There was no bay window from which to pontificate, no gaming room where deep play was held nightly. It owed no allegiance to either political faction, nor did its members routinely make or break social reputations.

The appeal of the Explorers' Society was in its disdain for all things fashionable. Those who were allowed to join were asked to observe three simple rules. It was never permissible to discuss politics or religion upon the premises. Gambling at cards for small stakes was permitted, but there was no betting book, nor games of chance. And quarreling publicly with another member was grounds for immediate expulsion.

In return, the club provided excellent dinners, a decent wine cellar, and a haven for like-minded gentlemen to retreat from the pressures of London society. And, from time to time, in a nod to the reason why the club was originally founded, the members would get together to finance some brave soul who wished to explore the unknown territories of the Earth. These hardy explorers were seldom heard from again, which was why the membership confined its own explorations to the reading of books and magazines.

Stephen Wright, the Viscount of Endicott, had inherited his father's membership in the club, along with his title. In the years since he had reached his majority, he had come to appreciate the club as the one place where he could retreat from the cares of the world and his own responsibilities. At least for a few hours.

Often he came here when he was worried, but today he was in a positively cheerful mood as he leaned back in his chair and crossed his long legs in front of him. In one hand he held a newly purchased account of the exploration of the Amazon River, while in the other he held a glass of excellent French brandy. A small decanter stood on the table beside him.

He opened the book and began to read. He was halfway through the first chapter, where the author was still recounting the lengthy preparations he had made for his journey. Two dozen crates of lemons and limes to prevent scurvy seemed a bit excessive, Stephen mused. Personally he would be more worried about preparing for attacks from wild creatures or the savage tribes who were said to live along the shores of that great river.

"Stephen, I am glad I found you," Anthony Dunne said as he took the seat opposite.

Lord Endicott looked up from his book. Anthony Dunne was a friend from Cambridge and normally a boon companion. But today his face held an unusually grim expression.

"Tony, what is it?"

"I need to speak to you."

Stephen used a ribbon to mark his place and then set the book aside.

"Are you well? Is there something wrong?"

"It is not me."

"Then, is it Elizabeth? Young John? Your mother?"

"Elizabeth sends her regards, and she and John are in excellent health," Tony said. He paused to rub his forehead with his right hand, a sure sign of agitation. "It is your family that we need to discuss. Your brother, actually."

Stephen breathed a sigh of relief, glad that there was nothing wrong with his friend's family. Indeed, Tony's wife, Elizabeth, was as close to him as a sister, and their five-year-old son, John, was his godson.

And troubles involving his own brother George, while occasionally distressing, were nothing new.

"You might as well tell me what it is," Stephen said, when Tony showed no signs of speaking. "Though I am certain it is not as serious as you make it out. After all, have you not heard the news? My brother has done us all a great favor. He and some friends left England yesterday, off to join the throng in Belgium, hoping to witness Napoleon's final defeat. From there they intend to tour the Continent. With luck they will be gone a year or more and can make fools of themselves in some foreign land."

In fact, Stephen had been celebrating that very news. Tranquil months stretched before him, with nothing to do but to attend to his own well-regulated affairs. No upsets, no scandals, no frantic pleas from his stepmother to rescue her son from the consequences of his own follies. No creditors asking for payment of George's bills, no irate fathers accusing George of fleecing their sons at the gaming tables.

No wincing when he opened the newspaper, afraid to see his brother's name linked to the latest scandal.

For such had been Stephen's lot in life these last four years, ever since George had made his appearance in London society, at the ripe age of seventeen. And in that time he had become very fond of the sanctuary of this club. The Explorers' Society was one of the few places in London where he could go and not expect to be confronted by news of his brother's latest peccadilloes.

Until today, that was. Now his brother's transgressions had intruded upon the peace he had found here.

"I think I know why George left," Tony said, giving him a look of sympathy that made Stephen tighten his grip on his brandy glass.

Stephen nodded. "Go on."

"It seems there was an incident. An incident involving a young lady of quality."

Tony paused a moment to let the implications sink in.

"Let me guess. The girl was ruined?" Stephen asked. He was proud of how steady his voice sounded, since he wanted to scream.

"Yes," Tony said. "Well, that is her reputation is ruined for certain. Whether your brother took more than a few casual liberties is—"

"Is not a matter I care to consider," Stephen said.

He had known George was reckless. Headstrong. Heedless of consequences. In the four years that George had been on the town, he had gone from one mishap to another. He had acquired a reputation as a rake, but never had he trifled with an innocent. Never had he crossed that final line that would put him beyond the pale of polite society.

Never until now.

"Her name is Miss Somerville. Her family is from Kent, and her reputation was unblemished until the night of Lady Payton's ball, when she disappeared from the ball with George and his friends. She returned home the next afternoon."

"And how do you know this?"

"Merely by happenstance. Elizabeth's dresser has a cousin who was employed as Miss Somerville's maid. When Miss Somerville disgraced herself, the father fired the poor girl. I suppose he had to have someone to blame. The dresser asked Elizabeth if she could find a place in our house for the maid and explained the circumstances. And so Elizabeth told me."

"And you came to tell me," Stephen said.

"Yes. I knew you would want to know. It is not yet common gossip in society. But in time I knew the story would come to your ears and thought you should hear it from a friend."

"I would rather have heard it from my brother. Or at least his side of it," Stephen said. But that was an old complaint. His brother never spoke to him, unless it was to request an advance against his allowance or to sneer at Stephen's unfashionable tastes and pursuits.

"George may, indeed, have an explanation. It could be that the gossip has wronged him," Tony said. But his face indicated that he did not believe his own words.

"Or the gossip may be true, in which case my brother has wronged an innocent," Stephen countered. "I owe it to myself to find out the truth."

"And then?"

"And then we will see," he said.

It took Stephen two days to piece the story together, a task made all the harder because he did not generally mingle in society, and his presence now would only serve to add fuel to whatever gossip was already brewing. George was the social one of the family, whose presence could be counted on at every significant event of the season, unless, of course, his circumstances had forced him to rusticate in the country until he could wheedle another advance on his allowance from his doting mother or disapproving elder brother.

Stephen, by contrast, preferred the company of his

friends, or places such as the club, where he could be certain of intelligent conversation. He was not a hermit, precisely, but left to his own devices he would far rather enjoy a quiet dinner at the Explorers' club than endure the crush of some rout or public ball.

However, his years of experience in dealing with his brother's troubles stood him in good stead. A morning call upon Lady Jersey gained him confirmation that Miss Somerville had left London in suspicious haste, having disgraced herself in some fashion. Though when pressed, Lady Jersey confessed that she did not know the details of the young lady's disgrace, Miss Somerville being too insignificant a personage to be thought worthy of her attention.

That night he spent going from one gaming hell to another in search of one of George's friends who might be able to provide information. He found a handful of young wastrels who admitted knowing his brother, but all denied any knowledge of his recent activities. Indeed, two had the impertinence to press him for payments of debts that George owed, something Stephen refused with a simple lift of one eyebrow. It was well known that George habitually outran his allowance, and if these fools had chosen to gamble with him, well, that was their own misfortune.

The next afternoon he went to White's Club in search of Mr. Arthur Fox, one of George's closest friends. Stephen had met him on several occasions this past winter, always in the company of his brother, George. Like George, Arthur Fox was a younger son who had chosen a life of idleness and dissipation. He played heavily at the gaming tables, relying upon his indulgent father to settle his debts. But unlike Stephen's other cronies, Arthur Fox had stayed in London rather than traveling to the Continent.

As Stephen entered the gaming room, he saw Arthur Fox bite his lip in concentration as he stared at the cards in his hand. There was a small pile of chips next to his left elbow, and a large glass of wine sat in front of him.

The pile of chips in front of his opponent was much larger.

"Well, young Fox, what is it to be?" Sir Maurice Howland asked, impatiently drumming the fingers of his left hand on the table.

"Mr. Fox chooses to fold," Stephen said.

Arthur Fox looked up. "But, Lord Endicott—"

"I say, you cannot do that," Sir Maurice Howland declared, sticking his chin out belligerently. "Not done at all."

"Mr. Fox chooses to fold," Stephen repeated. "He has a prior engagement with me, do you not?"

He caught and held Arthur Fox's gaze, until the young man gulped and nodded.

"Yes, sir. That is, Sir Maurice, if you would permit—" Arthur Fox stammered.

"I am sure as a gentleman you understand these matters," Stephen said, addressing Sir Maurice Howland. It would take all afternoon if he allowed Arthur Fox to try and make his own excuses. "This will not take long. Should you wish to wait, I am certain Mr. Fox would be happy to return to this table, and to give you opportunity to strip the last of his pocket money from him."

The tip of Sir Maurice's ears turned bright red, though whether it was from anger or shame, Stephen did not know.

"There are plenty of gentlemen here who would be honored to sit at my table," Sir Maurice said.

"Of that I have no doubt," Stephen replied. Indeed, an unholy passion for gambling in all forms was practically a requirement for membership in this club.

"Come now, Mr. Fox, and let us go somewhere we can speak privately," Stephen said.

Though he was not a member, his title and reputation, not to mention the gold coins he had pressed in the footman's hand, had secured Stephen the use of a small anteroom. The footman bowed them into the room, and as the door shut behind them, Arthur Fox flinched.

"Sit," Stephen said. "I won't bite you."

Arthur Fox did as he was told, looking far younger than the twenty years of age he claimed to hold. Stephen, who was approaching thirty, felt positively ancient when he looked at this wet-behind-the-ears cub.

"It is about the bet, is it not?" Arthur Fox asked, leaning forward slightly and clasping his hands nervously.

Stephen was confused, but decided to play along. "What makes you say that?"

"I did not do anything," Arthur Fox said. "I mean I was there when we made the wager. We all were. But I was drunk at the time. Once I sobered up, I knew I could never go through with it. I mean, I have sisters of my own, you see?"

"But the others decided to see the bet through."

Arthur Fox nodded. "George, Frank Patterson, and Harry Driscoll agreed to go forward. When I refused, they called me a flat, a hen-hearted milksop. I told them it was wrong, but they would not listen."

"And George won the bet?" Stephen asked.

He wondered what the precise terms of the bet had been.

"Yes. He picked that chit who was making cow eyes at him. Took her to some inn, then the next morning sent her back to her parents, as calm as you please. He brought some kind of proof, to show he had won. I wouldn't look at it, but I think the others did."

Stephen felt a slow rage begin to build in him. This was even worse than he had feared. If Arthur Fox was to be believed, the girl was not simply disgraced; she had been ruined. "And it did not occur to you to warn this girl? To warn her family?"

"I did not think he would actually do it," Arthur Fox said.

Stephen stared at him in disgust. The young whelp had the audacity to look miserable, when he was as much to blame for this mess as any of them. Too honorable to go through with the wager, but too faint-hearted to warn the young women that they were being stalked as prizes in some twisted game.

"And if it had been your own sister? What would you say to a man who had known of a scheme to ruin her, but chose to keep his silence?"

Arthur Fox's face turned white, but his voice was steady as he replied. "I would despise him for a coward," he declared.

Stephen looked at him hard, and Arthur Fox bore his gaze steadily. There was more backbone here than he had thought. Perhaps there was still time for Arthur Fox to mend his ways.

"Take a good look at yourself and decide if this is the kind of gentleman you wish to be," Stephen advised. "London is full of bad influences, my brother among them. If I were you, I would leave the distractions of London and not return until I was certain I could return as my own man."

"You are neither my brother nor my father," Arthur Fox said with a trace of his earlier defiance.

"For that I am grateful," he said. "Tell me one more thing and I will set you free, to find your own ruin if you must. The lady in question, she was Miss Somerville, was she not?"

"I believe so. George called her Diana, if that helps."

"Indeed, it does." Stephen rose from his seat. He had a sudden urge to leave this place and its unwelcome revelations far behind him. "I advise you not to speak of this to anyone else. Miss Somerville's reputation has been damaged enough; there is no need for you to add your share."

"Of course not," Arthur Fox said. "You have my word."

For whatever his word was worth. Still, there was no point in quarreling, so with a curt nod, Stephen bade him farewell and then made his escape from White's.

It was not till later, when he reached the privacy of his own rooms, that he allowed himself to think through the implications of what Arthur Fox had said.

It was no wonder George had fled to the Continent. He had been wise to fear Stephen's wrath. George's earlier scandals had been excused as the result of high spirits or reckless immaturity, his conduct no worse than many a young blade who frequented London society.

But now George had gone beyond mere indiscretion. This time he had deliberately set out to hurt another human being—to cause harm—in pursuit of an obscene wager.

Even now, no doubt Miss Somerville was mourning the ruins of her reputation, the loss of her maidenhead, and with it any hopes for a decent marriage. He could picture her quite clearly in his mind. Petite, with blond hair and blue eyes now swollen and red rimmed with crying.

Destroying an innocent was the act of a monster. If he had been able to lay his hands upon George, he would have beaten him to within an inch of his life.

But George had wisely chosen to place himself beyond his brother's reach. No doubt he hoped that in time Stephen would find it in his heart to forgive this sin as he had forgiven so many before. In time society, too, would forget the particulars, and should George return, he would have only added to his reputation as a rakehell.

But Stephen would not forget. Would not forgive. One day George would return, and on that day he would get what he deserved.

And there was a certain guilt in him as well. How much of the responsibility of this mess was his? Had Stephen's past indulgences only encouraged George in his willful misconduct? Perhaps if he had been stricter with George when George first came to London. After that first scandal with the duke's mistress, Stephen should have insisted that George make his apologies and accept banishment from London until the scandal had died down. But he had given in to Caroline's tearful pleadings, allowing his stepmother to convince him that George was truly sorry and would mend his ways.

Instead, his younger brother had careened from one scrape to another, and nothing Stephen said or did seemed to have the slightest influence. Indeed, his very disapproval seemed to only encourage his brother to even wilder acts.

And now there was Miss Somerville to consider. Miss Somerville, who might even now be carrying his brother's child. He would have to find some way to make amends to her and to her family for the harm his brother had wrought.

In such a situation there was only one honorable course of action. Marriage would resolve everything, in the eyes of society. If George had the least shred of decency, he could be made to see his fault and to know that there was only one course of action. He would have to offer himself in marriage to pay for his transgressions.

But he could not count on George to do the honorable thing. Even if his brother had not fled England, it was doubtful that Stephen would have been able to convince him to make an offer of marriage. Not when George's actions so clearly indicated that he had no intention of taking responsibility for what he had done.

So, it was up to Stephen to make amends. To offer

himself in place of his brother. Even the mere news of their engagement would be enough to restore Miss Somerville's reputation. And once married, she would have the protection of his name and rank.

Not to mention a father for any baby that might come. Indeed, if they were married swiftly enough, there would be no one to question the baby's paternity. Even Stephen, himself, would not know if he was raising a son or a nephew.

It might not come to that, he consoled himself. The Somervilles might have already arranged a quiet match for their daughter, finding an amiable gentleman who was willing to accept a wife with a blemished reputation.

Or they might be horrified by his proposal and refuse to have anything to do with the brother of the man who had ruined their daughter.

Most likely, though, they would be grateful for his offer and hastily accept lest he change his mind.

But in the end, what mattered was that he had to make the offer, to restore at least some portion of his family's honor. Whether she chose to accept it or not was Miss Somerville's decision, and he would agree to be bound by her wishes.

Two

Lord Endicott paced back and forth in front of the fireplace. The sitting room was the best the country inn had to offer, but it was not large and seemed to get smaller with every moment that ticked by.

Six paces to the wall. Turn. Six paces back. Three more paces and he stopped, clasping his hands behind his back as he gazed at the burning coals. Would Mr. Somerville even respond to his message? Would he think it impertinent? Would it have been better to call upon him at his residence? He had thought that a meeting here, on neutral territory, was less likely to give offense. But now, as the moments passed, he realized that summoning Mr. Somerville to meet with him, when by rights it was he who should be calling upon the other, might be seen as arrogance.

There was a double rap on the door, and then it swung open, revealing a middle-aged gentleman with a ruddy complexion, his black hair liberally streaked with white. Next to him was the innkeeper.

"Here he is, Mr. Somerville, the gentleman that is expecting you," the innkeeper said. "Shall I bring you gents summat to drink?"

Mr. Somerville glanced at him. "The cider here is quite fine," he said.

"Cider it is, then," Stephen replied.

The innkeeper nodded and bustled off.

Mr. Somerville had a kindly face, with laugh lines around the eyes and mouth. He looked like an altogether decent man. Now that he was face-to-face with the father of the woman his brother had so wronged, Stephen's palms began to sweat, and he felt a queasiness in his stomach.

"Mr. Somerville, I thank you for coming so swiftly," Stephen said.

"Lord Endicott, I do not believe we have met before," Mr. Somerville observed.

"No, we have not."

"Then, it is an honor to make your acquaintance," Mr. Somerville said as he advanced across the room and offered his hand.

The gesture surprised Stephen, but he hesitated only an instant before taking it and shaking his hand.

"I assure you, the honor is mine," Stephen said. He had not expected to be greeted so civilly. After a moment, he realized that Mr. Somerville was unaware of who he was. Or, more to the point, of who his brother was.

"Do our families know one another?" Mr. Somerville asked.

Stephen was saved from having to reply by the innkeeper, who bustled in carrying two pewter tankards of cider. As he left, Stephen closed the door firmly behind him.

"Please have a seat," he said. He waited until Mr. Somerville had sat down before taking his own seat.

Mr. Somerville took a long draught of the cider, and Stephen sipped at his own for politeness sake before setting it aside.

"Our families are acquainted, although under unfortunate circumstances," Stephen said, by way of explanation. "This is why I wrote to ask for the courtesy of a private interview with you."

Mr. Somerville put his cider aside. "Why do I have the feeling that this is not a pleasant topic?"

He could delay his errand no longer. "My given name is Stephen Frederick Wright, and I am Viscount of Endicott. My brother is George Wright."

He waited for the explosion of anger, but none came.

"I do not recall a George Wright," Mr. Somerville said.

How could he not know the name of the man who had ruined his daughter? Had George sunk so low as to use a false name? Or maybe this was all some impossible mix-up. Could there be more than one Miss Somerville?

"Your daughter is Diana Somerville, is she not? Who disappeared from Lady Payton's ball under questionable circumstances?"

Mr. Somerville placed the tankard down on the wooden table with a solid thud. "I fail to see what concern that is of yours, sir," he said.

So this was the right family. The father was angry, but he had not denied the events of that evening. It was time for some truths of his own.

"Then, you must know that when she left the ball that night, it was with my half brother, George. George Wright."

Mr. Somerville gazed down at the floor for a moment. When he looked up, he appeared ten years older than he had just a moment ago. "Stubborn chit never told us his name. Did not explain anything really. Just said she was sorry for causing a fuss."

Sorry for causing a fuss. "Are you saying she went with him willingly?"

If she had gone with him willingly, then that changed everything. If she bore at least some of the blame, then there was no need for Stephen to sacrifice his bachelor status.

"Of course not," Mr. Somerville barked. "Diana is a decent girl, properly raised. No, she said she was sorry she had trusted someone who was no gentleman. But she refused to tell me his name. Said she feared I might call him out or some such nonsense."

The brief hope that had flickered within him died. It was as he feared. George had, indeed, ruined this girl, much as Mr. Fox had related.

"I cannot tell you how sorry I am that this happened," Stephen said.

"And why isn't your brother the one here, making a pretty speech and begging my forgiveness? As if I could forgive the man who ruined my daughter."

"George left England over a fortnight ago. Before I knew anything of what had happened," Stephen said. But even if George had stayed, it was unlikely that Stephen would have been able to force him to do the right thing and to make his apologies.

"And is he likely to return?"

"To be blunt, I have no idea what my brother's plans are," Stephen said, letting the bitterness he felt color his voice.

"So your brother's the black sheep," Mr. Somerville said. "Happens in most families, from time to time. You have come here and said your piece, and now it is done with."

Mr. Somerville drained his tankard and then stood up, preparing to leave.

"That is not all," Stephen said. "I came to ask your permission to speak with your daughter."

"Why? So you can make your apologies to her as well? I see no reason to disturb her with such. Your brother is the one at fault, not you. It was decent of you to come here, but there is really very little you can do."

Stephen knew he could accept Mr. Somerville's dismissal and walk out of this room a free man. He could go back to London and resume his life, and the Somerville family would think none the less of him.

But he would think less of himself. He still felt at least partially to blame for not having acted sooner to curb George's wildness. And thus, the sense of honor that had driven him here insisted that he go forward with his original plan.

"On the contrary, I think there is something I can do," Stephen said. "With your permission, I would like to ask your daughter to marry me."

Mr. Somerville gaped at him openmouthed. "Diana? To marry you?" He sat down heavily and then reached across the table and pulled Stephen's barely touched tankard to him, taking several deep gulps of the sweet cider. Then he took out his handkerchief and began to mop his brow.

"You are generous, my lord, but that would never do. No, she would not stand for it," Mr. Somerville declared, once he had regained his composure.

"Why ever not?" Stephen asked. He felt positively insulted. Here he had come prepared to do the noble thing—to sacrifice himself—though many persons, his friend Tony Dunne included, would argue that such was far beyond what anyone else would expect him to do in the name of honor. Mr. Somerville should be expressing his heartfelt gratitude, not staring at him in disbelief.

There was nothing wrong with him. He was a viscount of England, after all, a far better catch than his wastrel brother. His appearance was unremarkable, his fortune good, and his reputation unblemished. What possible objection could the young lady have to him?

"Do you have any sisters?" Mr. Somerville asked, folding his handkerchief carefully and stuffing it back inside his breast pocket.

"No. There is just my brother." And even that was one sibling too many.

"I have daughters," Mr. Somerville said, leaning forward as if confiding a secret. "Seven of them. Plus my wife. A house of females it is, and I the lone rooster surrounded by cackling hens. Is it any wonder that I come to the Green Inn, from time to time, to drink Bob Jones's cider in peace and quiet?"

At some point the conversation had taken a turn for the bizarre, and Stephen was left to follow as best he could.

"I suppose any man in your circumstances would feel the same," Stephen said.

Mr. Somerville nodded emphatically. "Precisely. Just think of it. Seven daughters, all of whom will have to be taken to London and launched upon society. And Diana, the eldest, is the worst of the lot. Setting a bad example for the others, with her stubbornness and her outlandish ideas. Not that I do not love her. I do, you know. But what is a man to do when his daughter declares that she has no intention of being married? Instead, she plans to explore the jungles of Africa or some such nonsense. I mean, what would you do?"

"I have no idea, sir," Stephen said. The jungles of Africa? The Diana Somerville her father described was very different than the woman of his imaginings. He had expected her to be like George's other inamoratas, pretty, shallow, and more than a trifle vain. But it seemed that Miss Somerville was cut from a different cloth. An original, as it were. Imagine, a woman proposing to explore Africa. She was either very brave, very foolhardy, or quite likely both.

"But you have no objection to my meeting with her to offer her marriage?" Stephen asked.

"No, of course not. I will give you my blessings, and what is more, I will wish you the best of luck. Not that it will do you any good," Mr. Somerville said. "Once Diana has made up her mind, a team of horses could not budge her from her course."

"We shall see," Stephen said.

He could be stubborn as well where matters of his honor were concerned. No matter what her father said, he found it unlikely that Miss Somerville would reject.

Not, that was, until she was certain that there were no consequences from her encounter with George.

He would meet with this Miss Somerville and hear from her own lips what she wished from him. And if Miss Somerville declined the honor of becoming Lady Endicott, then he would take his leave and count himself fortunate.

Stephen arrived at the Somervilles' residence at half past two. A footman showed him into a small study, where Mr. Somerville sat reading.

"You are late," Mr. Somerville said, closing his book and glancing up at the clock. "Thought you had changed your mind."

"No," Stephen said, "though I apologize for the delay. It was unavoidable."

He knew he was late, but it was not his fault. Not really. If there were any fault, it lay with Josiah, who had been impossibly slow this day.

After lunch, Stephen had donned formal attire, as befitted such a solemn occasion. A dark blue coat of superfine, pants of the same fabric, striped waistcoat, snowy white linen shirt, and black shoes polished to a mirror shine. Five cravats had been ruined in trying to achieve the perfect knot. But then, regarding his appearance in the mirror, he had decided that he looked too stiff. Too formal. It might appear as if he were trying to impress Miss Somerville with his elevated status.

So he had changed, donning instead buckskin trousers, a bottle green jacket, and butter-soft riding boots.

Ordinary attire, as if this were an ordinary social call. Three more cravats were ruined trying to create a more casual knot, until Josiah finally took pity on his master and tied it for him.

Glancing at Mr. Somerville, who still wore the frock coat he had worn this morning, Stephen felt glad he had decided to appear in his less formal garb. It was a simple matter of courtesy, really, not wishing to outdo your host. It had nothing to do with his wanting to make a good impression on this Miss Somerville.

"Shall I send for Diana?" Mr. Somerville asked.

"If you would be so kind."

He waited, standing by one of the bookcases, idly perusing the titles as the footman was dispatched in search of Miss Somerville. He felt nervous as only a man can be when he realizes that the next few minutes might very well decide the rest of his life.

"Papa, can this not wait? I was busy helping Emily with her paints."

A woman entered the room, and Stephen blinked in surprise. She was tall, slender, with dark black hair that was piled in a knot on her head, from which tendrils had escaped to curl down the sides of her face. There was a smudge on the end of her nose, and he fought the urge to wipe it away.

"Papa?" she asked, her eyes darting in Stephen's direction.

Mr. Somerville rose to his feet. "Diana, this is Stephen Wright, the Viscount of Endicott. George Wright's brother. Lord Endicott, this is my daughter Diana."

Miss Somerville drew herself up to her full height

and looked him directly in the eye, a thing few women could achieve. "I have nothing to say to this man. Nothing," she repeated, dismissing him with a scornful glance. She spun on her heel and prepared to leave.

"Diana!"

At the sharp command her steps faltered, and slowly she turned around.

"I have promised this gentleman he may have five minutes of your time," her father said. "As this is still my house, and you are my daughter, you will grant him that courtesy. Is that understood?"

"Perfectly. Five minutes and no more," she said, enunciating every word clearly. Her blue eyes shot daggers at Stephen.

"I wish you luck," Mr. Somerville said, clapping one hand on Stephen's shoulder. Then he left, shutting the door behind them, and they were alone.

Now that he was in her presence, Stephen did not know what to say. The carefully rehearsed speeches flew out of his head, leaving his mind a blank. Finally, realizing that she was waiting, he began to speak.

"Miss Somerville, I came to apologize to you for the injury my brother has done to you."

"I wish to have nothing to do with you or, indeed, with any member of your family. You are not welcome here. If you wish to please me, you will leave. At once."

She was angry. That much he had expected. And with George far distant, Stephen was the only target for her wrath.

"I came to make my apologies on behalf of my family. And to offer you a way out of this situation. A way to redeem your name and restore your reputation." He took a deep breath and then said the words that were irrevocable. "Miss Somerville, I ask you to do me the honor of becoming my wife."

He held his breath, awaiting her answer.

Miss Somerville blinked. She had uncommonly fine eyes, he noticed.

"Mad. You are quite mad," she said, with a decisive nod.

It was the second time today that his suit had been dismissed as unworthy of even a moment's consideration. His pride could not bear such an insult.

"Mad? You are the one who is mad. Any other woman in your position would leap at the chance to reclaim her reputation. Not to mention the chance to become a viscountess. Not a bad bargain for a night's work."

Her cheeks colored, and a sudden wave of shame washed over him.

"I beg your forgiveness," he croaked. "I do not know what came over me. I had no right to speak such words."

"At least it proves you are human, after all. Such nobility must be hard to live up to," Miss Somerville said.

He risked a glance and to his surprise found that she was regarding him not with anger, but rather studying him quite seriously, as if he were a rare beast at the zoo.

"George spoke of you often," Miss Somerville said.

"I doubt it was flattering."

"He said you were stiff with honor. At least he got

that part right," Miss Somerville said. "After all, George is the sinner here, and yet you came all this way to offer to marry me. Payment for your brother's crimes as it were. I think most would say that is carrying nobility a bit far."

She crossed the library and sat down on a small sofa. At her nod, Stephen took his own seat on a brocaded chair opposite. The chair creaked alarmingly as he sat on it, and he wondered if it would hold. Having the chair collapse under him would complete his utter humiliation.

"I bear at least some of the blame for George's misconduct," Stephen said. "If I had been able to curb his wildness sooner, this might never have happened."

"You are his brother, not his father," Miss Somerville responded. "And in truth, his sin is not so large as you seem to believe."

"But you. Your, er, your reputation is ruined," Stephen answered. He could feel his ears coloring, but he could hardly mention the loss of her maidenhead.

Miss Somerville shook her head. "The reputation does not matter. I had no plans to marry anyway. As it is, I look upon that evening as an educational experience."

"An educational experience?" His voice rose in disbelief. How could she be so blasted calm? "Are you saying you wanted him to make love to you?"

Now it was Miss Somerville's turn to blush. "Oh," she said in a small voice, her gaze firmly fixed upon her feet.

He followed her gaze and noted that the toes of her slippers were scuffed.

"Nothing happened," she said.

"Nothing?"

"No. Though he did try," she said, her gaze coming back to him. "But I told him if he touched me, I would cast up my accounts. He did not believe me, and so I was forced to carry through with my threat."

His mind boggled at the image her words painted. George, his face no doubt flushed with strong drink, preparing to take Miss Somerville's innocence by force. And Miss Somerville, defending herself with the only weapon she had. Her wits.

"I take it he was not pleased?"

"It seems I ruined a pair of satin breeches, not to mention his silk stockings," Miss Somerville said, smiling a little in remembrance. "He left me alone after that, although he refused to let me leave the inn where he had brought me. Not till the next morning, anyway, when he hired a hackney coach to take me home."

"But why did you go with him in the first place?"

"It was warm that night, and after we danced, Mr. Wright suggested we could cool off by taking a turn in the gardens. It was foolish of me, I know, but I thought of no harm, save perhaps that he might want to steal a kiss."

At this she blushed, and he realized that she felt guilty for her imaginings. But she was hardly to blame after all. A stolen kiss was a minor peccadillo when compared with attempted rape.

"You trusted him," he said.

"Yes. I thought I did. And if he had contented himself with a single kiss, then we would have parted as friends.

"Instead, once we were out of view of the others, he began to drag me toward the back gate. I should have screamed, but I did not want to cause a scene. I was sure I could make him listen to reason if he would just stop for a moment. Before I knew what was happening, he bundled me into a carriage that was waiting outside the gate. And the rest you know."

Or could guess.

"And you swear that is all he did?" Stephen asked.

"I swear. It was uncomfortable, and I was frightened, I will admit. But he did not hurt me in any way except my pride. I thought myself a good judge of character, until that night. Now I know better than to put my trust in a gentleman whom I barely know."

He knew he should be relieved. So George had not committed the ultimate sin, although it was not for lack of trying. If another woman had found herself in Miss Somerville's situation, no doubt she would have been ruined in fact as well as in name.

As it was, only Miss Somerville's reputation had suffered. The woman herself was still as she had been, an innocent. And there would be no consequences from that evening, no bastard child that needed the protection of his name.

"I am glad that he did not harm you," Stephen said. "But the damage to your reputation is harm enough. I regret to tell you that word of that night has already spread through London, and the gossips have made their own sordid conclusions. It is unlikely you will find a gentleman willing to overlook such a tale and marry you."

Which was a shame, since she really was quite a pretty girl. And a brave one, too, to have come through her ordeal unscathed.

"I have no intention of marrying. I am an advocate of women's rights and plan to live my own life outside of society's conventions," Miss Somerville said.

"Your father mentioned something of that sort. He said you wished to explore Africa?"

Miss Somerville shook her head. "Papa never listens to me. I have told him a hundred times. When I reach the age of one and twenty I will receive my inheritance from my great-aunt Sophie. And with it I will explore the world and become the most famous female explorer since Lady Hester Stanhope. I will start by being the first female to journey along the Amazon River."

"The Amazon River is in South America. Brazil, actually," Stephen said.

Miss Somerville's eyes sparkled. "Of course it is, though to Papa one foreign place is the same as any other. Do you know of it?"

"Yes," he said. "The Explorers' club financed an expedition there three years ago. I have just begun reading a book which recounts the story of the expedition."

"It must be fascinating."

He shook his head. "A dangerous place, to be certain. The chapter I just finished relates how one of the clerks fell overboard at night, and before he could be rescued, he was devoured by a school of predatory fish."

"A river shark?"

"No, it was described as a mass of small fish. Like brook trout, or even smaller. But a giant school that tore the poor soul apart as his companions watched helplessly."

It was not a pretty tale. Indeed, it was not one fit to be shared with a genteel young lady. But rather than looking appalled, Miss Somerville appeared fascinated.

"You must give me the name of the book," she said. "I wish to learn everything I can before I make my own voyages of discovery."

She would not last a week in the wilds of Brazil. Indeed, he was surprised she had lasted for a month of the London season. She was that most terrifying creature of all, an innocent who had no sense of self-preservation. No wonder her father had despaired of her making the logical choice and accepting Stephen's offer of marriage.

"That day is still some time away," Stephen said. "And in the meantime, there is still your reputation to be considered."

"I have said I do not care for it," Miss Somerville replied. "I only went to London to make Mama happy. I have no wish to return."

"You have younger sisters, do you not? Six of them?"

"Yes. Mary is a year my junior, and then there is Chloe, Julia, Elizabeth, Annabelle, and Emily is the youngest. She has just turned eight."

"Then, it is not just your reputation that will suffer," Stephen said. "When Mary makes her curtsy to society, your conduct will reflect upon her."

He did not know why he was doing this. A part of him knew he should accept her refusal and simply take his leave and count himself lucky on making his escape. But he could not do that. Whether she knew it or not, Miss Somerville was a true innocent and in need of his protection. Now it was up to him to convince her to accept it.

"Surely once they get to know Mary, they will realize that she is a sweet and biddable girl and judge her on her own merits," Miss Somerville said. But her voice lacked conviction.

"Society is swift to judge and slow to forget," Stephen said. "They will look at Mary and wonder how long it will be before she follows her sister down the road of indiscretion."

"Then, what do you suggest? I will not marry you," she declared.

But he had expected that. "We do not need to be married. A simple engagement will suffice. Then in six months' time, your father will send a notice to the papers calling it off. Society will assume that you have changed your mind, and they will be none the wiser."

"And this is what you want?"

He did not know what he wanted. The path of duty and honor had seemed so clear this morning. But that had been before he met Miss Somerville. Now he was no longer certain of anything.

"Honor demands I do no less," he said, falling back upon platitudes.

Miss Somerville looked at him steadily, as if she could see through to his very soul. He forced his face to remain calm, revealing none of his inner doubts.

"Then, I agree. But we will tell my parents of the pretense. I will not have them disappointed when I break this off," Miss Somerville said.

He breathed a sigh of relief. "To make this work, we will have to appear in public together. It would be best if you returned to London."

"I suppose it would not hurt. A few weeks should suffice, and then we can return to our separate lives, and everything will go on as before," Miss Somerville said.

"It will be as you wish," Stephen said.

Three

Papa took the news of her sham engagement in good spirits, commending her on showing good sense for once. Perhaps he was simply relieved that lasting scandal could be averted. He had been very good about the whole affair, really. Well, except for when he had fired her maid, thinking that poor Sally was somehow to blame. But even there he had relented, eventually agreeing to send Sally two months' wages for her troubles, along with a fine letter of recommendation. But all in all, he had been far kinder to her than many a father would have been. Some fathers would have beaten their daughters for having ruined their good name, regardless of the daughter's innocence.

But, as Diana had expected, her mother was confused about the whole arrangement.

"I do not understand," Mama said. "Are you to be married or are you not?"

"Mama," Diana began. "It is all perfectly plain. You see—"

"If I may," Lord Endicott broke in smoothly. "Miss Somerville has agreed that I may tell the world of our engagement. That should squash any unfortunate rumors that may be spreading. Then, come autumn, should she wish to be freed from her promise, I would of course accept her decision."

"I see," Mama said, her brow furrowed in thought. "A sort of trial engagement as it were."

"Precisely," Lord Endicott said.

Mama nodded, as if the viscount had made everything clear with his words, when Diana had been trying unsuccessfully to explain the very same thing for the past quarter hour.

"And if Diana decides she wishes to marry you after all?" her father asked.

"Don't talk nonsense," Diana said firmly.

Lord Endicott looked at her and lifted one eyebrow, as if taken aback by her blunt speech. "If she chooses to go forward with this marriage, then it would be my honor to become her husband."

Now it was her father's turn to nod and stroke his chin thoughtfully.

Really it was most infuriating. For years she had been presumed capable to speak for herself. And now this stranger was in her home for barely an hour, and merely because he was a gentleman, her parents listened to him respectfully and deferred to his wishes. Simply because he was a man. This was why she was so opposed to marriage. Mary Wollstonecraft was right. Marriage was a trap for a woman, taking away her rights and subjecting her to the capricious will of her husband. No intelligent female would enter into such an institution unless forced to by the pressures of society.

She had half a mind to call this whole engagement off. But then she remembered Mary. Her sister was as conventional as she was pretty. Mary dreamed long-ingly of her own London season and the handsome beaus who would court her there. Diana did not understand her sister, but she loved her dearly. If the sham engagement would restore Diana's reputation and let Mary enjoy her own season, then she would go through with it.

There would be time enough for Diana to live her own life after Mary was safely launched upon society. And once Diana left England upon her adventures, there would be no risk of her younger sisters being tarnished by anything that Diana might choose to do.

"We are fortunate that it is only May, and that the season has several weeks to run," Lord Endicott was saying. "Once we return to London there will be plenty of time to establish the fact of our engagement."

"But I do not want to go to London," Diana said. She knew she sounded like a whining child, but she spoke only the truth. Even before that disastrous night, she had not enjoyed herself in London. The other young ladies had been cruel to her once they learned of her outlandish views. And the gentlemen her mother's friends introduced her to were inevitably straight-laced and boring, or young men so full of admiration for themselves that they barely noticed that Diana was in the same room with them.

George Wright had been the exception. From the first she had thought him a kindred spirit. A free thinker, who rebelled against the petty tyrannies of polite society, just as she longed to do. His reputation was not the best, but she had put that down to narrow-minded gossip. His attentions had surprised her, and she had flattered herself that he was attracted to her for her mind. And then, of course, he had proven that he was naught but a lecherous rake.

"If we are going to do this, we must do this right," Lord Endicott said. "A short stay in London should suffice. We will make our appearance at a few public events, and then when the season is over, we will part our ways."

"For myself, I have no wish to return. And we have already given up the lease on the house," her father said.

But Lord Endicott had anticipated that objection. "There is no need to trouble yourself," he said. "I have a house on Chesterfield Hill that should suit your needs. It is a good size, with a half dozen bedrooms and a large drawing room should you wish to entertain. And the staff is excellent."

She wondered why a viscount would happen to have a house in London that he was not using in the height of the London season when fashionable properties were as scarce as hen's teeth.

"Is it your mistress's house?" Diana asked.

"Diana Somerville," her mother exclaimed, blushing at her daughter's impertinence.

But Lord Endicott grinned, an expression that made him look years younger. Diana realized that he was actually a handsome man.

"It is mine, actually," he explained. "But I will move back to the family residence in Grosvenor Square. It is much larger and will be suitable for our engagement ball."

She felt control of the situation slipping away from her. "I did not agree to a ball," she said.

"It is expected," Lord Endicott explained. "And London will not be so bad. There are museums and exhibitions that you may attend. Not to mention that Henry Richman is planning a series of lectures on his experiences in the Amazon."

"Is he the one that you were telling me of?"

"Mr. Richman led the exhibition, yes. It was his assistant, an unfortunate gentleman named Watkins, who was eaten by the carnivorous fish."

Diana beamed happily. "I cannot wait," she said. "I have a thousand questions I want to ask him."

Lord Endicott rose. "Then, it is settled. I will send the notice to the papers and alert the staff at Chesterfield Hill to expect your arrival," he said.

Stephen returned to the inn in a thoughtful mood. He still did not understand why he had insisted so strongly that Miss Somerville agree to the pretense of an engagement. And yet, having seen her, he could not imagine simply leaving her, knowing that she would bear the brunt of the scandal that George had caused. She was too good a person to deserve such a fate.

As he entered the room assigned to him, his valet, Josiah, looked up from the stack of freshly laundered cravats that he was pressing.

"Congratulate me, Josiah, I am to be married. I think," he said.

Josiah looked up at him from under his bushy eyebrows, but did not pause in his ironing. "And what does the young lady say to all this?"

"The young lady has her doubts," Stephen said. There was no point in keeping secrets from Josiah, who knew him as well as he knew himself. "But she has agreed to announce our engagement, to give the scandal time to die down."

"And Master George?"

Stephen's mood darkened at the reminder of his half brother. "My brother's behavior is not a topic I care to discuss," he said. "Let us just say that the miserable cur is fortunate that he is far out of my reach, for I am sorely tempted to teach him a lesson he would never forget."

Indeed, if George were to appear at the door this moment, Stephen would be hard pressed not to thrash his brother to within an inch of his life. Not that such a beating would do anything to curb George's wildness or restore Miss Somerville's reputation. But still, there was a primitive part of him that longed for such satisfaction.

"I plan to stay here for another day or two and become better acquainted with my fiancée and her family," Stephen said. If they had any hope to carry off the pretense of an engagement, then they could not afford to appear as complete strangers. No, instead, this must appear to be a love match. "When the Somervilles return to London, I will go with them."

"It is a good thing I packed for a week, then," Josiah observed.

"Yes," Stephen said. "I need you to ride to London tomorrow. I will give you notices to be sent to the newspapers. And you will go to Grosvenor Square and tell Higgins to open up the viscount's apartments. I will be taking up residence there for the rest of the season, while the Somervilles stay in the town house."

Josiah shook his head. "Your stepmother will not like having you in her house."

Indeed, Stephen and his stepmother, Caroline, had never been fond of each other. Not since he was a young lad of seven and his father was exhorting him to be kind to the lady who was to take the place of his own mother. They had detested each other at sight, and the birth of her own son, George, had only served to cement Caroline's dislike for her husband's eldest child. Over the years he had learned to disguise his dislike under a mask of formal politeness. But even his father had recognized the tension, and when Stephen turned twenty, his father had presented him with the house on Chesterfield Hill, enabling him to set up his own residence.

When his father had died two years later, Stephen had briefly contemplated moving into the house in Grosvenor Square, but he had soon decided against that. Caroline's influence was felt in every room of the house, and it seemed too cruel for him to ask the newly made widow to vacate the house she had loved so well.

Seven years had passed, and Caroline was still firmly entrenched in Grosvenor Square. Indeed, she hardly ever left London, where she played the role of a fashionable widow to the hilt. She ignored Stephen entirely, unless there was something she wanted from him, and then she would send for him, crying pretty tears and begging him to take care of her, painting herself as a poor widow, left helpless by his father's untimely death.

There had seemed no good reason for him to challenge the status quo, but now his engagement gave him the perfect excuse to assert his rights.

"My stepmother has reigned as Lady Endicott long enough," Stephen said. "It is time I took control of my inheritance. This will give her time to get used to the idea. After all, when I do marry, she will be forced to give precedence to my bride."

"She is not going to like it," Josiah repeated.

"Then she can leave," Stephen said firmly. "Since she is so attached to her son, she can join him in Brussels."

Or there was the dower house in Eastbourne which had been left to her outright, not that he expected her to tamely accept such banishment. But even the threat of such should be enough to ensure her compliance should she prove difficult over his presence in what she perceived as her household.

Not to mention what the news of impending marriage would do to her composure. For he had no intention of telling Caroline that the engagement was merely a ploy. Let his stepmother suffer a little, believing that her reign as Lady Endicott was about to end. It would be fitting punishment for her role in this debacle, since she bore her own share of blame for the flaws in George's character.

Four

Papa invited Lord Endicott to stay with them as their guest, but the viscount politely refused and, instead, stayed at the inn for the two days it took for Papa and Mama to prepare for the return to London. He behaved most civilly, as if he were, indeed, a suitor come to visit his intended's family. He dined with them that first night and spent the evening playing draughts with her sisters.

The next day he accompanied her on a stroll through the village and then spent the afternoon closeted with her father in his study. When she asked what they had discussed, her father had said only that they were discussing the terms of the engagement. Which was ridiculous. What was there to discuss? It was not as if they truly intended to go through with this marriage.

But perhaps Lord Endicott simply wished an escape from the females of the household. Though he was too polite to say so, she sensed that he found himself overwhelmed by the Misses Somerville. Certainly it was unlikely that he had ever before sat down to dine at a table with eight women and only one other gentleman.

On the morning of the third day, they left for London. As the carriage rolled down the driveway, her sisters waved energetically and shed copious tears, some of sorrow and some of envy.

Diana rode with her parents in the hired carriage, while Lord Endicott chose to ride his horse alongside. He saw to all the details of their travel arrangements, and under his management the journey was accomplished with remarkable ease. When the carriage broke a wheel, rather than becoming angry or frustrated, Lord Endicott simply took charge. He sent the coachman for help and in a short time had arranged conveyance to the nearest village. There they dined in a private room at the posting inn, while the village smith repaired the wheel. By the time they were done with their lunch, the carriage was ready for them. All arranged in quiet efficiency and with little fuss.

Really, her fiancé was a very useful sort to have around. The type that would be handy to have in a crisis if one were traveling in the uncharted wilderness. Though he seemed to lack the adventurous spirit required to undertake such journeys. So unlike his brother in so many ways. With George she had felt an instant connection. Within mere moments of meeting they had been chatting away as if they were old friends.

With Lord Endicott it was different. He was always polite, of course, but underneath there was a reserve that kept the world at a distance. From time to time she would find him gazing at her, when he thought she was unaware. Such looks made her uncomfortable. They made her feel as if he was judging her. And she could not help wanting to know what he thought of her, though she knew by now that even if she asked, he would not tell her.

On the evening of the second day, they reached London, and Lord Endicott guided the carriage through the busy streets to the town house at Chesterfield Hill. Their arrival had been expected, for the windows were ablaze with lights. As the carriage drew up to the stairs, the front door opened, and servants hurried out to open the carriage door, while others began unloading the luggage.

Lord Endicott dismounted, and as a servant held his horse, he accompanied them inside.

"This is Mr. Barnes, the butler, and his wife, Mrs. Barnes, the housekeeper. They will see to your comfort," Lord Endicott said. "And these are the Somervilles and their daughter Miss Diana, who is to be my wife."

Diana blinked in surprise, but fortunately no one seemed to notice. His wife. It sounded strange, but she supposed she would have to get used to it.

"It is an honor to have you here," Mr. Barnes said.

"Come now, you must be weary after all that jolting around in the carriage," Mrs. Barnes said, helping Mrs. Somerville remove her cloak. "Let me show you to your rooms. The maids are bringing hot water for washing, and then there is supper waiting for those that are hungry."

Suddenly hot water and the prospect of a soft bed sounded incredibly wonderful to Diana, as if she had been traveling for two weeks instead of a mere two days.

"I will leave you in Mrs. Barnes's capable hands," Lord Endicott said. "Miss Somerville, may I call upon you tomorrow afternoon? Perhaps we could take a drive in the park, if you are not too fatigued."

The viscount was wasting no time. In the afternoon the park was certain to be crowded with members of society. It would be their first public appearance and a chance to see if society accepted the fact of their engagement.

"That would be lovely," Diana said.

"Until tomorrow, then," Lord Endicott replied, and with a bow to her parents, he departed.

"How could you do this to me? Have you no regard for my feelings?" the dowager Lady Endicott demanded. She had pounced upon him the moment he entered the Grosvenor Square residence, practically dragging him off into the Chinese parlor, with its crimson-and-gold-patterned walls and vast collection of tasteless oriental knickknacks.

"Good evening, Caroline," Stephen said. *Yes, the journey was pleasant. Yes, I am well,* he said to himself, but he knew she had no interest in such subjects.

"You made a fool out of me," Caroline said. She stuck her lower lip out in a pout. At the age of seventeen it might well have been attractive. Now that she was perilously close to forty, it only made her look ill-tempered.

Not that his stepmother looked old. On the contrary, she had retained her slender figure. In a candlelit ballroom, with her still-golden curls and carefully rouged cheeks, she might well pass for a woman of thirty. It was only in the sunlight that her true age showed, just as it was only with her family and the servants that she allowed her shrewish nature to appear.

She was dressed uncommonly finely, in a low-cut evening gown of the finest French silk. No doubt she was planning on going out that evening. It was a shame that she had not already left.

Stephen sat down and stretched his legs out before him. After two days in the saddle, he wanted nothing so much as to strip off his clothes and sink into a hot bath. But he knew from long experience that Caroline would insist on having her say. Better to get this over with now.

"What have I done to upset you?"

Caroline stood over him, glaring, and then whirled away, the fabric of her gown swirling around her. "You made me look like a fool. Today, at Mrs. Hendrick's breakfast, that harpy Louise Richman insisted on being the first to congratulate me on the good news. Of course, I had no idea what she was talking about. Imagine my mortification when she revealed that the notice of your engagement had appeared in the morning papers."

Stephen sighed. "I trust you managed to escape with your dignity intact?"

Caroline sniffed. "Of course. I am no green girl, after all. I told Mrs. Richman that it was a long-standing engagement, and I was merely surprised, having expected the notice to appear next week."

Stephen nodded. "That was clever of you."

"But it was all your fault. You could have told me. You owed it to me to tell me first. I am your father's wife, after all."

His father's wife. George's mother. That was all she had ever been to him. Not once in the past twenty years had he ever been tempted to call her Mother. He swallowed against the sudden bitterness that rose in his throat.

"I sent a letter with Josiah. Did you not read it?"

Caroline shrugged, waving one bejeweled hand. "If he gave me such a thing, I do not remember it. Really, I was in such a pet when he told me you intended to open up your father's apartments. I knew it must all be some sort of dreadful mistake. Those rooms have not been used in years. I cannot possibly expect to get them ready. Josiah tried to insist, but I sent him packing."

Stephen sighed again and closed his eyes, pinching the bridge of his nose with his fingers. He could feel a headache coming on.

"You sent him off," he repeated. "My valet."

"Yes. I knew it was all a hum. Why would you want to stay here, when you have your own perfectly adequate town house?"

Caroline dimpled at him prettily, as if he were one of her cicisbei. Her smile slipped as he maintained his silence.

"My fiancée, Miss Somerville, and her parents are in residence at Chesterfield Hill," he said, summoning up his patience. "And as for this house, I believe it is mine as well. It is high time that I took up residence here. And it is perfectly suited for hosting a ball to celebrate my forthcoming marriage."

His stepmother was silent, and he could not resist adding, "Do not worry. We do not plan to be married until the autumn. There is no need for you to vacate the viscountess's apartments until then."

He took a certain satisfaction in seeing Caroline's face pale as his words sank in. Really, she was quite a foolish woman, and for the ten thousandth time, he wondered what his father had ever seen in her.

Caroline had been so caught up by her affronted dignity that she had not realized what his engagement meant to her. On the day he married, there would be a new Lady Endicott. A woman who would reign as mistress here at Grosvenor Square, as well as at the family estate in Eastbourne. Caroline would be relegated to the position of dowager viscountess, and a guest in her stepson's home.

"The season is nearly over. I cannot possibly arrange a ball on such short notice," Caroline objected.

"I beg to disagree. I was thinking of the second week of June, and that should give you more than sufficient time to plan such an event," Stephen said. "Of course, if you find the task beyond you, I am certain I could rely upon Miss Somerville and her mother to make all the necessary arrangements."

"There is no need for that. If you insist upon this folly, then I will do what is necessary. And I will not have another woman running my house," Caroline said.

"This is my house, as you may recall," Stephen said. "And I do insist." Which was a rarity in their relationship. In the past it had always been easier to let Caroline have her own way in all things. There had been few things that he wanted strongly enough to challenge her over. But this was different.

"And this young woman? Do I know her? What of her family?"

It was clear that whatever gossip was circulating had not yet reached Caroline's ears. Which was strange, for he knew she was friends with some of the most avid gossips in London. Then again, even such ladies would no doubt have hesitated before telling Caroline of a scandal involving her beloved son. Not to spare her feelings, but more because they knew she would not believe them.

"Miss Diana Somerville is a young woman from a good Kentish family—an original really—and I know you will find her quite charming," he said. He hoped Caroline was intelligent enough to heed the subtle warning in his words. He would tolerate no unpleasantness from her toward Miss Somerville.

"She sounds dull," Caroline said. "Is she pretty at least?"

"Very," he said, though he had not given the matter much thought before. Still, as he conjured up her image in his mind's eye, he knew he was right.

"And how did you meet such a paragon?"

Stephen smiled. "If it were not for George, I would never have met her."

Caroline stared at him openmouthed in surprise.

"And now, if you will excuse me, I need to wash off the dust of the road," he said.

"You cannot stay here," she said. "Your father's rooms are not ready."

There were a dozen bedrooms in the house, but no doubt if he inquired, she would claim that none of these were suitable either and blame the lackadaisical staff. When the truth was far simpler. He tasted bile again as he wondered which of her lovers she had been entertaining in the rooms that had been his father's. No doubt she wished him gone so she could remove all evidence of her indiscretions.

"I will stay at the club tonight," Stephen said. "But you can tell the servants that I will be returning tomorrow. And if all is not in readiness, I will begin asking questions until I find the reason why. Is that understood?"

"Perfectly," Caroline said. "And there is no reason to take such an uncivil tone. I am only thinking of your comfort."

The day Caroline gave a thought to his comfort was the day that hell would freeze over. And with that bleak thought, he bade her good night and took his leave, before he said anything that would permanently sever their relationship. Not that he cared for himself, but Caroline's public support would be vital to ensure the success of the engagement. A quarrel with her now would serve no purpose. He had endured her scorn and contempt for years; another few months were no great burden to bear.

But after the engagement was over, he would make it clear to Caroline that he was no longer prepared to turn a blind eye to her indiscretions. Nor would he allow her to blithely rule over what, by right of inheritance, was his. He had indulged her and his half brother long enough, with disastrous results. Now it was time to reclaim what was his.

Five

"I still do not understand why you feel compelled to go through with this sham engagement. You said yourself that Miss Somerville's virtue is intact. Surely there was no need for such drastic measures," Tony Dunne said.

Stephen shrugged. How could he explain what he himself only half understood? "It seemed the right thing to do."

After all, it was clear that George had intended to seduce Miss Somerville. Forcibly, if necessary. Only her quick wits had saved her. And even then, George had done his best to blacken her reputation, providing his cronies with so-called proof that he had won the wager by taking a young lady's innocence. Someone had to protect her, and there was no one else willing or able to take on the task.

"I do not like this," Tony Dunne said. His face was still troubled, and he rubbed one hand over his chin. "I wish you had spoken to me first, before you went to Kent."

Stephen had known that Tony would be upset to see the news of the engagement in the newspapers, which was why the morning after his return he had come to call upon his friend. But unlike his stepmother, Caroline, he knew that Tony's distress came from genuine concern and the fear that his friend had done something rash, something that would turn out badly for all concerned.

"What if this girl changes her mind and decides she wishes to be a viscountess in truth? What will you do then, if she refuses to break the engagement?" Tony asked.

"Then we would be married, of course," Stephen said. He had always known such was a possibility from the moment he had made his offer. Strangely the thought did not distress him, although he could understand why Tony Dunne was concerned. Then again, Tony had yet to meet Miss Somerville.

"But I doubt very much that such will come to pass," Stephen explained. "I do not meet Miss Somerville's requirements for a husband."

Tony lifted one eyebrow. "And those are?"

Stephen shrugged. "I am entirely too conventional for her tastes. Respectable. Conservative. Dull, one might say. But my greatest failing is that I have no wish to drag my wife on a trip through the jungles of India or the wild rivers of Brazil."

"India? Brazil?"

"Miss Somerville wishes to be the next female explorer, following in the footsteps of her idol, Lady Hester Stanhope. She feels a husband would be an impediment to such a career, but if she had to choose, I am certain she would choose a gentleman who shared her interests. Not someone like myself, whose only explorations are done in a comfortable armchair while sipping port."

"You value yourself too little," Tony chided him.

"On the contrary, I am a realist."

"And how do you plan to make this scheme work? If this Miss Somerville is as you describe, it will be difficult to pretend that the two of you have formed a love match," Tony said.

"Society will see what they expect to see," Stephen said. "A few public appearances should suffice. And as for Miss Somerville, I find that I like her. She is honest, which is a refreshing change from most women of the *ton*. Once you know her, I hope you and Elizabeth will learn to call her friend as well."

"You can depend upon us," Tony said. "For whatever you need."

"Thank you," Stephen said. It was something he had known, just as he knew that he would do anything for his friends. And yet there was a certain comfort in hearing Tony say the words aloud.

"I am to begin this afternoon by taking Miss Somerville for a drive in Green Park," Stephen said. "Then I suppose it is time I begin accepting some of the invitations that have come my way."

Indeed, although Stephen rarely attended social functions, he was nonetheless bombarded by London hostesses, each of whom hoped to claim the honor of attracting the elusive viscount. Now he would have to change his habits and let society see him and his fiancée.

"Elizabeth suggested that we could host a small dinner party to introduce Miss Somerville to our friends,"

Tony said. "Perhaps Friday or Saturday, if that would suit your plans."

Today was Tuesday. It was late to send out invitations for such an event, but then again Elizabeth Dunne was a peerless hostess. No doubt she had already considered such before making her suggestion.

"That is most kind. Please tell Elizabeth I accept her generous offer."

"And shall we tell anyone else the real story of this engagement?"

"No," Stephen said. He had given this much thought. It was not that he did not trust his other friends, but there was a limit to how many could be expected to keep a secret. "You may speak to Elizabeth, if you think it wise, but no one else. A secret shared is soon no secret at all."

"I will tell Elizabeth," Tony said. "I learned early in our marriage never to keep a secret from my wife. That is advice you would do well to heed, if you are considering matrimony."

"I am a long way from making a husband," Stephen said. "First, I must practice the part of being a fiancé."

At the appointed hour Lord Endicott arrived, driving a fashionable curricle drawn by a matched pair of bays. A footman helped her into the carriage, which swayed alarmingly as she took her seat next to the viscount. Then, with a smart crack of the whip, they set off.

Diana clutched her straw bonnet with one hand and resisted the urge to clutch the viscount with the other. Far lighter than the sturdy gigs she had ridden in at home, the curricle seemed almost flimsy, balanced precariously upon its two wheels, as it was pulled by a matched pair of horses. Never before had she ridden in such a daring vehicle, nor been driven quite so fast. She swallowed nervously, feeling slightly queasy at the swaying of the curricle. But then she began to relax as she realized that the viscount was a very competent driver. He navigated the busy streets of London with great skill, weaving in and out among the congested tangle of coaches, horse carts, and pedestrians.

"There is no need for worry. The curricle is far safer than it looks, and I have never overturned a vehicle I was driving," Lord Endicott said, after a sidelong glance.

"I am not frightened," Diana said. "In fact, I am intrigued. I have never ridden in a curricle before."

"And how do you like the experience?"

"It is interesting," she said. She wondered how fast the horses could pull such a lightweight vehicle and wished for an empty country lane so Lord Endicott could put them through their paces.

"A new experience for you, then," Lord Endicott said. "An adventure as it were."

"I would like to learn to drive," Diana said, voicing aloud the thought that had just occurred to her. "Perhaps someday you can teach me?"

"It is more difficult than it appears," Lord Endicott said. "And Hector and Ajax here are very well trained, which makes my part look all the easier."

Diana bit her lower lip as she often did when thinking. "I have driven the pony cart at home," she said. "And as an adventuress I will need all sorts of skills.

What if someday I encounter bandits and my coachman is wounded or killed? I may be called upon to drive my own carriage to safety."

She found herself lost in visions of her future heroism. It would be in the Italian Alps, or perhaps along a desert trail in Arabia. She would win against enormous odds, driving the carriage to safety and acquiring universal acclaim. Newspaper correspondents would rush to pen her story, and her friends and family back in England would be astonished at her daring.

Lord Endicott interrupted her daydream. "I do not believe there is any risk of us being attacked by bandits between here and Green Park. Especially not on a sunny Tuesday afternoon in May."

The poor man had no imagination whatsoever, she realized. No wonder he was so stiff and formal. She must remember to make allowances for him. It was not his fault that he could not share her vision. He was simply blinded by the limits of convention and of long habit.

"If you had an adventurous soul, you would understand. But I realize that is not your fault. Not all of us were born to lead exciting lives," Diana said. She reached over and placed her hand comfortingly along his arm.

Lord Endicott looked down at her hand and then over at her, until an indignant cockney yell brought his attention back to his driving.

"I thank you for understanding my limitations," he said, his voice stiff. "And I did not say that you should not learn to drive a carriage. If you do intend to travel, it will be a useful skill to have. But a curricle is not a carriage, and the streets of London are no place for a novice to learn."

"Then, you will teach me?"

"We shall see," Lord Endicott said.

She sank back against the cushions. He had not agreed, not exactly. But neither had he refused her.

"Smile," he said.

"What?"

"Smile," he repeated. "That gate ahead leads to Green Park. It is time to begin our performance."

"Oh," she said. She had been so intent upon their conversation she had almost forgotten the true purpose of this outing.

Lord Endicott slowed the horses to a walk as they passed through the gates onto the carriageway. The park was positively filled with people, some strolling along the grass, while carriages of every kind and condition made a stately procession along the carriageway. There were high-perch phaetons and gaily painted curricles, along with ancient carriages and a few light gigs. Lord Endicott nodded to acquaintances, who nodded back to him. A rider on horseback drew up alongside them, touching the brim of his hat with his whip.

"Endicott. A fine afternoon for a drive, is it not?" The speaker was a fashionably dressed gentleman wearing a pale blue coat over doeskin trousers, with sandy blond hair and a fair complexion.

"Indeed," Lord Endicott said, drawing the curricle to a halt. "May I present Miss Somerville, who is to be my wife. Miss Somerville, this is Mr. Harold Walker, who was at Cambridge with me."

"Delighted to make your acquaintance, Miss Somerville," Mr. Walker said, giving a very credible bow for one who sat in the saddle.

"A pleasure, sir," Diana replied.

"It has been a long time since we last met. One despairs of seeing you in society," Mr. Walker said. "Does your presence here mean that you plan on changing your hermit ways, now that you are engaged?"

A muscle in Lord Endicott's jaw jumped, but then he smiled affably. "My fiancée and I will of course be delighted to take part in the season," he said. "And now, if you will excuse us, I do not wish to keep the horses standing."

"Of course," Mr. Walker said. "Miss Somerville, I look forward to improving our acquaintance."

Diana smiled and inclined her head, but said nothing. She had not liked the subtle mockery in Mr. Walker's voice. She waited until they had driven some distance down the path before saying, "I do not think Mr. Walker is your friend."

"He is not. He is an acquaintance," Lord Endicott said.

"And is it true? That you never venture into society?"

"I am not quite the hermit that Mr. Walker claimed," Lord Endicott answered. His gaze was fixed ahead. "But it is true that I lost my taste some time ago for large crushes, or attending five parties in a single evening, simply because one must be seen at all the most fashionable events."

"I have little taste for such things myself," Diana

confessed. Though that was not precisely true. It was easier to lose oneself in a large crowd and to melt into the background. In a smaller party it was harder for her to remain in obscurity, while her unconventional views had brought her all too much attention, most of it unwelcome. In her brief time in London she had grown to loathe fashionable gatherings. In a way the scandal had been a blessing, for it had put an end to the season.

"It will be different now. For both of us," Lord Endicott said. "I no longer have to fear hostesses trying to force their giggling, hen-witted daughters upon me. And you will find that what was distressingly eccentric in Miss Somerville is considered merely charming and original in the future Viscountess Endicott."

His words were kind, but underneath them she heard a bitter cynicism. Or perhaps simply weary resignation. After all, Lord Endicott had been an eligible bachelor for years now. Perhaps he was tired of feminine wiles and stratagems, and that had prompted his retreat from society.

"And when the season is over?"

"Then there will be no need to dissemble," he said.

His answer left her curiously unsatisfied, but there was no time to question him, for another voice demanded their attention.

"Miss Somerville," a woman's voice called out.

Diana looked, and saw Lady Spenser and her daughter, Joan, being driven in a gig.

"Miss Somerville," Lady Spenser called out again, waving her parasol.

"That is Lady Spenser," Diana said. "I know her, slightly."

"And I know her well," Lord Endicott said under his breath. "Or rather her reputation. She is a gossip, and precisely what we need."

He maneuvered the curricle so it was off the path, drawing it up alongside the gig.

"Lady Spenser, Miss Spenser," he said. "I trust I find you well?"

"Very well, indeed," Lady Spenser said.

Her daughter, Joan, clasped her two hands in her lap and stared down at them, her face obscured by the wide brim of her bonnet.

"I must congratulate you, my lord, and you, too, Miss Somerville," Lady Spenser said. "We were so pleased to read of your engagement. Weren't we, dear?"

She poked her daughter in her side, and Joan Spenser lifted her head. "Most pleased," she whispered.

"I thank you both," Diana said.

She felt sorry for the girl. She had spoken with Joan Spenser a few times, when they both found themselves wallflowers at one of the many balls. Miss Spenser seemed like she would be a nice girl if she were ever allowed to escape from her mother's domineering influence.

"Thank you," Endicott said.

"Some of your acquaintances were surprised by the suddenness of the announcement," Lady Spenser said. "And, of course, when we wished to offer you our congratulations, we found you had left London."

There was a speculative gleam in Lady Spenser's eyes, and Diana had a nasty suspicion that this horrible woman knew everything. She knew that the engagement was a sham and that Diana's reputation had been hopelessly compromised. Why had she agreed to this madness? They were never going to be able to fool the *ton*. Never.

Lord Endicott came to her rescue, reaching over and taking her hand in his. He gave her hand a gentle squeeze.

"We were in Kent, of course," Lord Endicott said. "Naturally, I wished to make myself known to Miss Somerville's family. She has six sisters at home, who were not able to join the family in London. It seemed fitting that they make my acquaintance before the notice appeared in the newspapers."

"Of course," Lady Spenser said. "But you must admit it seems rather sudden. I was not even aware you knew one another."

"Our families are acquainted," Lord Endicott said. "And as for myself, I was never one to make my business public. Not until I knew for certain that Miss Somerville would have me."

Every word he said was true, and yet at the same time they also served the deception. Their families had known one another, for she and George had been acquainted. And he had come to Kent to meet her family, though he had come to make his apologies and not as a suitor. At least not initially.

He gave her a conspiratorial smile, and Diana found herself smiling back. She realized Lord Endicott was very good at this game of deceiving with the truth, and she wondered what other surprises were hidden behind his reserved facade.

He bent his head down toward hers, and for a brief moment she thought he was about to kiss her.

"Ahem," Lady Spenser said, clearing her throat.

Lord Endicott lifted his head with a guilty start, and Diana felt her own cheeks flushing.

"I see. A love match, as it were," Lady Spenser said. Her lips were pursed as if she had tasted vinegar.

"I am very fortunate," Lord Endicott said.

"As am I," Diana echoed.

"Again our congratulations," Lady Spenser said. "And now we must take our leave, before our carriages become affixed to the spot."

She tapped the driver on his shoulder with the tip of her parasol, and the driver obediently coaxed the horses into a walk.

"That went very well," Lord Endicott said. "By tomorrow morning Lady Spenser will have told half of London of our return to town. No doubt she will assure everyone that it is a love match, and she, and she alone, was privy to the secret of our courtship."

"But why would she say that?"

"Because she wishes to puff up her own consequence by claiming to be the only one who knows the true secret of our engagement. And a love match is a far more interesting story than a mere marriage of convenience."

"And will the rest of society accept us as readily?"

"If we play the part," Lord Endicott said. "Show them what they expect to see, and in time they will forget that there was ever any whiff of scandal attached to your name. Indeed, they will forget that you were ever paid court by George."

"Then, I will do my best," Diana said. Though it was already hard to remember that it was only a part. There had been that moment there when she had felt such a clear connection to him, only to have the spell broken by Lady Spenser.

Her mood had unaccountably turned dark, and she tried a jest to lighten it. "I will have to be on my mettle. You, sir, are clearly wasted in the House of Lords. Your talents belong on the stage."

"On the contrary, I will match Parliament against Drury Lane any day for histrionics and dramatic performances," Lord Endicott said.

He pointed with his whip, and she saw that they had once again looped back toward the entrance gate. "Shall we call it a day? I believe we have been on display long enough."

"I second that notion," Diana said. Indeed, she had much to think about.

Six

They had been in London for five days now, and Diana Somerville was still adjusting to her new status. On Tuesday, Lord Endicott had taken her driving in Green Park. On Wednesday, they had toured the larger, more fashionable Hyde Park, exchanging polite greetings with other members of the *ton* who had gathered to show off their finery and enjoy the pleasant day. For someone who claimed to rarely mix with society, Lord Endicott certainly had a wide circle of acquaintances.

On Thursday, her mother had held an at home, having sent notice of their new address to her acquaintances in London. The house had been thronged with callers come to offer their congratulations and inspect the future Viscountess Endicott. It was fortunate, indeed, that the viscount had offered them the use of this house and its excellent staff. Their former residence, while respectable, would never have held even one quarter of those who had come. As it was, Diana felt very much on exhibition, forced to smile and nod as middle-aged women congratulated her mother on her good fortune in firing off her eldest so successfully. Meanwhile, their daughters none so subtly questioned Diana, trying to discover the stratagems by which an insignificant country miss had captured the eye of such an eligible nobleman.

After three hours of such nonsense, Diana was heartily glad when the last of the callers had left, and she felt a new sympathy for the beasts displayed at the Royal Menagerie.

On Friday, Lord Endicott suggested another drive, but Diana had had enough of being on display. Instead, she proposed a trip to the bookseller's, and after a moment of consideration he agreed. He had even gone so far as to present her with a copy of Sir Henry Richman's account of his adventures on the Amazon, much to her delight.

Now it was Saturday, and they would make their first formal appearance as a betrothed couple, at a dinner party to be hosted by his friends. As the evening approached, Diana found herself growing more nervous. It was one thing to deceive strangers, or those whose opinion she cared little about. But these were Lord Endicott's friends. Would they not see through the deception? And, if they did, what would they think of her for agreeing to this sham?

"I do not like this," Mrs. Somerville said, as she came into Diana's room. In her right hand she held a jewelry case, covered in worn green velvet.

"What don't you like, Mama?"

"This. All this," Mrs. Somerville said, waving her unencumbered hand in a gesture that encompassed Diana, and her gown hanging on the wardrobe door.

Diana frowned. They had visited the dressmaker earlier in the week, but of course none of the gowns she had ordered were ready yet. Instead, they had altered one of the gowns made earlier in the season, replacing the plain white bodice with one of primrose satin, which contrasted nicely with the white silk skirt. She had thought the gown quite sophisticated, but now she had her doubts.

"Is it too plain? Perhaps I should wear the lilac silk instead, or is that too formal?" Diana asked.

"The gown is fine. You will look lovely," Mrs. Somerville said. "It is the deception I do not like. Pretending to our friends and acquaintances that you and the viscount do indeed plan to be wed. And now tonight we will begin to deceive his friends as well."

"The engagement was Lord Endicott's idea," Diana reminded her mother. "Surely he has thought through all the consequences."

"And do his friends know you are only playacting at this engagement?"

"He did not say. For now, we must assume that only the four of us are privy to this secret. You, Papa, myself, and Lord Endicott. As far as the rest of the world is concerned, Lord Endicott and I are no different from any other couple that is pledged to wed."

"I do not like this. I was never any good at secrets," Mrs. Somerville repeated.

Indeed, her mother had a distressing tendency to blurt out the truth at the most inconvenient of times. Whether it was Mary's infatuation with the son of the vicar, or Diana's surprise gift for her father's birthday, no secret was safe with Mrs. Somerville. Her daughters had learned the perils of confiding in their mother at an early age.

It would have been far safer to leave her mother in

Kent, but that would have begged too many questions. And yet each day her mother was here increased the risk that her mother would accidentally reveal their deception.

Diana thought furiously. It was time to take a page from Lord Endicott's book and bend the truth to fit their purposes.

"It is not a deception, Mama. We would not ask you to lie. Lord Endicott and I are truly engaged to be married," Diana said.

Mrs. Somerville regarded her doubtfully. "You are engaged, but you do not plan to be wed."

"That does not matter," Diana replied. "We will not be the first engaged couple to part ways at the end of the season. What matters for now is that we are engaged, and you can tell your friends and acquaintances so with a clear conscience."

"And if I am asked about the wedding?"

"Tell them we have not set a firm date. That we are still making our plans," Diana advised.

"I will do as you say," Mrs. Somerville said. "But this all would be easier if you were to marry Lord Endicott in truth. I don't suppose—"

"No, Mama," Diana said firmly. It would be cruel to encourage her mother in false hopes. She knew her mother wanted her to be happy, but she also knew her mother believed that such happiness was best found with a kind husband and a family of her own.

It was time to change the subject.

"There was a reason you came to see me?" Diana asked, indicating the jewel case.

"Oh, yes," her mother said. She walked over to the

dressing table and put the case on top of it. Opening the lid, she reached in and withdrew a pair of garnet earrings that glittered in the late afternoon sunlight.

"I thought these would go well with your gown," Mrs. Somerville said. "And there is a pendant to match."

"They are beautiful," Diana said, reaching her hand forward to touch the delicate jewels. Until now she had worn only the pearls her father had given her or the diamond earrings inherited from her great-aunt Sophie.

"They were a gift from your father when you were born," Mrs. Somerville said, smiling in remembrance. "William was so pleased he could hardly contain himself. You would think he had invented you."

"I will take good care of them," Diana said.

"They are yours now. Anyway, they will suit your coloring far better than mine," Mrs. Somerville said, touching one hand to her graying curls.

"Thank you," Diana said, swallowing around a suspicious lump in her throat. She wished for an instant that this was all real. That she was truly engaged to a man that she loved, and that her mother's gift was something that Diana, in turn, would pass on to her own daughter some day.

Lord Endicott called for them at seven, and Diana and her parents rode with him the short distance to the Dunnes' residence. They were the first to arrive, as Lord Endicott had no doubt planned. In her mind she had imagined that his friends would be much like the viscount, courteous, but reserved. To her surprise she found Mr. Anthony Dunne and his wife, Elizabeth, were two gregarious souls, who greeted the Somervilles as if they were old friends instead of newly made acquaintances. Within moments they were merrily chatting away, and by the time the guests began arriving, Diana had forgotten any trace of her nervousness.

Mrs. Dunne had described this as a simple dinner, but a full two dozen couples sat down at her table as the servants brought one lavish course after another. At the table, Diana was partnered on one side by Lord Endicott and on the other by an elderly Irish peer by the name of Lord Peter Quinn. Lord Peter nodded politely as she took her seat, but had little conversation, instead devoting his full attention to his plate.

Fortunately the Dunnes did not hold to strict formality, and conversation was general. She noticed that Lord Endicott seldom initiated conversation and, when addressed by the others, confined himself to the briefest of replies, stopping just short of incivility. Still, with so many lively conversationalists, she doubted anyone else would have noticed his restraint.

"Miss Somerville, I must confess the news of your engagement took me quite by surprise," Miss Clemens said, catching her eye from her seat across the table. "I had not thought you so fickle-minded."

Diana took a sip of her wine to cover her dismay. It had been too much to hope that no one would comment on the rumors that had linked Diana with Mr. George Wright.

And Miss Clemens had a powerful motive for stirring up trouble. Envy. After all, Miss Clemens was in her third season as one of the reigning toasts of London. Rumor had it that she had turned down dozens of eligible suitors, claiming that she was holding out for a title. No doubt she saw Diana's engagement to the Viscount of Endicott as a personal affront.

"Fickle?" Diana repeated.

"Why, yes," Miss Clemens said, with an artificial laugh. "I remember quite plainly the night of Lady Jersey's rout. You were telling all who would listen that the institution of marriage was a trap, and that no intelligent woman would be part of such. And yet now you yourself are to be married. Have you so changed your mind?"

She thought for a moment, hearing the other conversations fall silent as the company awaited her response. "I believe I said that the institution of marriage benefits men far more than it does women. When a woman marries, she gives up her independence and, indeed, all her legal rights. That said, I have no objection to a marriage where the partners enter into it with their eyes wide open and the intention of making a match of equals."

"And are these your sentiments as well, Lord Endicott?" Miss Clemens pressed.

Diana held her breath, wondering how he would respond.

"Only a fool would discount Miss Somerville's worth simply because of her sex. As for myself, I count myself lucky that she agreed to have me, despite my own flaws," Lord Endicott said.

His ready support pleased her, and she smiled at

him, willing to believe for the moment that he did, indeed, respect her opinions and that this was not all just part of their playacting.

"Gentlemen are poor creatures, indeed," Mrs. Dunne said. "Where would they be if we did not take pity on them?"

Mr. Dunne laughingly agreed, praising his wife for having the great kindness to marry him, and Diana breathed a sigh of relief as the conversation turned to less dangerous topics.

After dinner, the ladies retired to the drawing room, while the gentlemen enjoyed Tony Dunne's fine port. The talk soon turned to politics, but Stephen found his mind was elsewhere, wondering how Diana was faring.

Not that he did not trust Elizabeth Dunne to keep an eye out for her. But there were harpies aplenty in London society, as witness Miss Clemens and her insinuations. Even if Miss Clemens was hardly a match for Diana, who had put her in her place with a few choice sentences.

Still, it was a relief when the gentlemen finally rose to rejoin the ladies.

As Stephen entered the drawing room, his eyes were drawn immediately to Diana, who sat on the sofa, conversing animatedly with Mrs. Forsythe. Mrs. Forsythe was something of a bluestocking herself, and no doubt the two had much in common.

Stephen made his way through the room, paying his respects, until his footsteps drew him as if by accident to Elizabeth Dunne. He allowed her to pour him a cup of tea, though in truth it was far too late to drink such a beverage. Still, it gave him an excuse to linger, and he took a seat opposite his hostess.

"I think the evening is a success. As usual you have outdone yourself," Stephen said.

Elizabeth Dunne shook her head modestly. "It was only a simple dinner party. Nothing to fuss over."

"We gave you little time to prepare, and yet you still managed to plan the affair and assemble a respectable guest list."

Indeed, the guests appeared to have been very carefully chosen. Most of them were friends of his or the Dunnes, leavened with a sprinkling of the leaders of London society, such as Miss Clemens and her brother, Matthew. And if asked, all who dined here would recount the tale that there was nothing at all remarkable in the evening, which was precisely as they had hoped.

"It was not difficult to convince folks to attend," Elizabeth Dunne said. "Everyone was eager to meet your intended. As was I."

He raised one eyebrow. "And?"

"And she is not what I expected," Elizabeth Dunne said.

There was a strange heaviness in his chest, and Stephen schooled his face not to show the disappointment he felt.

"She is uncommonly intelligent and forthright," Elizabeth Dunne added musingly. "An original, in the truest sense of the word. I find I like her."

"I am glad," Stephen replied. He wanted his friends to like Diana. Which was strange, he knew, since the engagement was only a pretense.

"But she is not a woman I would have picked for you."

Ever since she had married Tony, Elizabeth Dunne had been trying to find a bride for his friend. She had introduced him to a score of eligible maidens: cousins, school friends, acquaintances from her home. Finally Stephen had had enough, and he had begged Tony to intercede for him. From then on the matchmaking stopped, although Elizabeth persisted in voicing her determination that what Stephen truly needed to secure his happiness was a wife.

"Under different circumstances we would probably have never met," Stephen said.

Elizabeth Dunne glanced around, making certain no one was near enough to overhear. "How on earth did she get mixed up with George's set? His reputation is well known, and surely she was not naive enough to fall for his wiles."

Stephen shook his head as a trace of the old anger arose. "Do not mistake intelligence for common sense. Miss Somerville is still quite the innocent, for all her vaunted learning. And I dare say if her parents had moved more often in society, rather than rusticating in Kent, they would have known enough to warn her of my brother."

"It was not your fault," Elizabeth said.

It was kind of her to try and absolve him from blame, but Stephen knew full well where the fault lay.

"What is done is done," he said.

"And what will you do this autumn? When she decides it is time to part ways?"

Diana's laughter rang out from across the room,

drawing his eye toward her. He had thought her pretty before, but now, seeing her cheeks flushed with laughter, he admitted that she was, indeed, beautiful.

Strange, he had known her for less than a fortnight, and already he felt protective of her. What would he feel four months from now, when it was time to let her go?

"By the autumn I will have plenty of practice at playing the part of a fiancé. When Miss Somerville decides to cast me off, perhaps I will let you give full rein to your matchmaking instincts and direct you to find me a wife."

"It will be difficult to find you another such original," Elizabeth Dunne said.

It would be impossible.

Seven

In the days after the Dunnes' dinner party, Diana and her parents were besieged with invitations to fashionable gatherings. Hostesses who had before disdained the Somervilles as insignificant country gentry now wrote to urge them to attend their routs, balls, Venetian breakfasts, musicales and a host of other diversions. It would have been flattering, but Diana knew that most of the invitations were prompted by the novelty of her engagement and the desire to count a future viscountess among their guests. It was not as if these women truly knew her or were interested in Diana's character.

But there were a few exceptions, friends she had made earlier in the season or new friends from Lord Endicott's circle, such as the Dunnes. These invitations Diana eagerly accepted. For the rest, she let her mother and Lord Endicott decide which invitations needed to be accepted and which could safely be ignored.

A few people had the poor manners to comment upon the suddenness of Diana's engagement, but they were in the minority. Indeed, some of those who knew that she had been seen with George Wright complemented Diana on her good sense. They, like Miss Clemens, seemed to think that Diana had used George

Wright and then discarded him in favor of his older and titled brother. Such insinuations infuriated her, especially since she could make no defense without giving away the deception.

Before she knew it, three weeks had passed, and she found that she and Lord Endicott were becoming an accepted part of the London scene. To her surprise she found herself enjoying her stay in London, as she had not earlier. It was different now that she was an engaged woman. No longer did she fear becoming a wallflower or finding herself trapped at a rout with no one to talk to. At Lady Sefton's ball, for the first time she found herself dancing every dance. She had expected Lord Endicott to claim the two dances that custom allowed, but was surprised to find other gentlemen eager to fill up her dance card. Perhaps, she mused, it was because the other gentlemen now considered her safe and had no fears that she would read anything into their attentions.

Lord Endicott continued to take his duties seriously. Indeed, she doubted he could have been more attentive if they were truly engaged. Though he did not see her every day, it was rare that two days passed without him calling at the town house or engaging to escort her to whatever entertainment was planned for that evening. Though she had resolved to maintain her distance from him, it proved impossible to do so. Despite their differences, the more time she spent with him, the more she came to think of him as a friend. And she knew she would miss his friendship when they finally called an end to this charade.

There was one thing that troubled her. Lord Endicott

had generously introduced her to his friends and acquaintances, so that she was now an accepted part of their social set. But she had yet to meet his stepmother, despite hints to Lord Endicott from both her and her parents that it was past time for such introductions to be made. She even suspected that Lord Endicott was purposely choosing social engagements where he could be certain they would not accidentally encounter one another, and yet that made no sense either. Why would he not want her to meet the dowager Lady Endicott?

The time for subtlety was past, and Diana resolved to broach the subject with him at the first opportunity, which came that afternoon when he arrived to escort her to a lecture by the newly knighted Sir Henry Richman, the intrepid explorer of the Amazon.

Diana was writing in her journal when she heard a soft knock. As she looked up, the library door opened, and Lord Endicott entered the room.

"One moment," she said, turning her attention back to her book. She finished the sentence with a flourish, then set her pen down and capped the inkwell. She carefully blotted the page before closing the precious book.

Through this process Lord Endicott watched her in silence. When she looked up again, there was a faint smile on his face. "Good afternoon, Miss Somerville, I trust I find you well?"

"Very well," she said. "And yourself?"

"I am fine," he said automatically. She realized she had never heard him admit to being otherwise. He was never bored, or fatigued, or anxious, or even excited.

He was always fine, as if admitting to anything else would be in conflict with the code of honor that governed his life.

"I had thought your parents were to join us?"

"Papa is otherwise engaged," Diana said. "I think he mentioned his tailor or some such. And Mama was to accompany us; indeed, she seemed quite amazed as I told her of Sir Henry Richman's exploits. But then, unaccountably, she developed a dreadful headache and is now resting in her room. She sends her regrets."

The faint smile ghosted across his lips again and was gone before she could be certain that she had seen it. "Then, I will have the pleasure of your company to myself," he said.

"While we are private, there is one thing I wish to speak to you about."

"And that is?"

"Is there some reason you do not wish me to meet your mother? We have been in London for nearly a month now, and it seems terribly rag mannered that we have not been introduced. I shudder to think what she must think of us."

Lord Endicott's face tightened. "My mother has been dead for over twenty years. And as for my father's second wife, I see no reason to inflict her acquaintance upon you. The less you have to do with her, the better."

The venom in his tone took her by surprise. It was so unlike his normally calm demeanor.

"But I do not understand. In less than a week she is to host a ball to celebrate our engagement. The invitations have all been sent out. Why would she do this and not wish to meet me?"

"You can rest assured that the ball was my idea and not Caroline's. But you should have no fears. As the dowager Lady Endicott, Caroline knows that her presence in the house at Grosvenor Square is conditional upon her acting as my hostess. And she has too much pride in her own reputation to let anything go wrong. The ball will be a success, she will see to that."

Lord Endicott turned, walking over to the window, so that his face was hidden from her. He ran the fingers of one hand along the globe that stood next to the window, and Diana was reminded anew that this was his house, filled with his possessions, for all that she and her parents now resided here.

"I do not understand. Is Lady Endicott upset over the deception? Is that why she does not want to meet me?"

Lord Endicott shook his head, then turned around so that he faced her from across the distance of the room. "She does not know it is a sham. Lady Endicott believes, as does the rest of London, that we are, indeed, to be wed."

"No," Diana said, rising to her feet. "I will not have that. We cannot deceive her in that way. I will not deceive her."

Lord Endicott's face remained cold and unreachable. "It is not your choice to make."

Diana crossed the room until she stood before him, close enough to touch him.

"But will she not be hurt when she finds out the truth?"

"On the contrary, she will be delighted when the engagement is called off," he said. "My dear stepmother very much enjoys the privileges of being Lady Endicott and has no wish to relinquish the title. No doubt she will hold another party to celebrate the end of our engagement."

The bitterness in his voice shocked her.

"I am sorry," she said. She realized she had misjudged the situation. Whatever the relationship between her fiancé and his stepmother, it appeared to have been a difficult one. Not to mention that Lady Endicott was the mother of George Wright, his errant half brother. Perhaps he blamed her for his younger brother's misconduct.

"In truth, these days I find myself very much tempted to be married," Lord Endicott said. "If for no other reason than the pleasure of casting my stepmother down from her lofty perch."

Diana could not repress a shiver. His words were cruel, and she found them hard to reconcile with the man she thought she knew. And she felt a certain sympathy for Lady Endicott. It must be difficult to be a widow and to be dependent upon your stepson for your very existence. It was another reason why many enlightened thinkers argued against the institution of marriage.

"Do not waste your sympathy on my stepmother," Lord Endicott said, as if he could read her very thoughts. "My father left her well provided for. Very well provided for, indeed, though she prefers to come cry upon my shoulder rather than to use any of her fortune to pay off her son's debts."

"I cannot judge a woman I have never met," Diana said. She was inclined to trust Lord Endicott, but she knew that there were two sides to any story. And Lord Endicott was hardly an unbiased observer.

"All I ask is that you reserve judgment until you have met her. Then you will see her pettiness for yourself."

"Now we are truly behaving as an engaged couple," Diana said, trying to lighten the mood. "For we have had our first quarrel."

"Let us hope it is our last," Lord Endicott said.

"It was during the third week of our travels upriver, on a Sunday evening, that I sensed our native guides were becoming restless. I summoned their leader, a fellow called Samuel, and asked for an explanation. In his broken English, he explained that one of the paddlers had seen an evil sign in the water, a warning that danger was near. Of course I dismissed this as so much superstitious nonsense. Indeed, I would have given the matter no more thought had that not been the night that poor Mr. Watkins fell from the boat into the river and perished. Were it not for my quick thinking, I dare say . . ."

As Sir Henry Richman droned on, Stephen turned his attention to Miss Somerville, who sat beside him in rapt fascination, her eyes shining as she took in every word. At least Mr. Watkins's death had been quick. Sir Henry Richman's victims seemed destined to perish from boredom as the self-aggrandizing lecturer continued his tale.

He glanced around and saw that Miss Somerville was not the only one entranced. Every seat in the assembly room was filled with folk eager to hear the firsthand account of the dangerous and exotic Amazon. And Sir Henry certainly knew his audience, for he played to their sensibilities, modestly deprecating his own abilities, yet somehow managing to make himself the hero of every incident he described.

If there was even a grain of truth to these tales, Sir Henry should have been killed a dozen times over, rather than living to return to London in triumph. Stephen wondered cynically just how far Sir Henry had ventured up the Amazon River, before turning back. A day? A week? He looked too pale, too well fed, to have endured the hardships that he described in such detail to his fascinated listeners, who hung on his every word as if they were gospel truth.

He suspected the unfortunate Mr. Watkins would have told a far different tale had he survived.

Stephen shifted uneasily in his seat, then glanced over, but Miss Somerville did not appear to notice his restlessness. Then again, he knew she was not in charity with him at the moment. Not after their earlier quarrel.

He knew he had handled that badly, but her innocent questions had touched him on a raw spot. And so he had let her see the anger he carried inside, anger he only rarely acknowledged even to himself.

No doubt Miss Somerville now thought him a prickly sort of fellow, easily stirred to anger. Perhaps she saw him as holding a grudge against the woman who had tried to replace his mother. And a part of that was true. As a child he had resented the beautiful young woman whom his father had brought into the house, a woman he was to call mother, but who clearly had no use for him. But as he had grown older, he had set that anger aside, only to find Caroline gave him new cause for grudges.

Stephen knew she had been unfaithful to his father, though he did not know if his father had ever realized that the wife he had doted on had made him a cuckold. Stephen had borne his knowledge in guilty silence. There was no sense in confronting Caroline, and he would not be the one to tell his father. Such knowledge would have only hurt his father and forced him to choose between believing in his wife or his eldest son.

After his father's death, Caroline had continued her affairs. Society was content to turn a blind eye as long as she did not flaunt her indiscretions. At least now she was no longer Stephen's concern, and he had ignored his stepmother to the best of his abilities.

But now circumstances had forced them together, and Stephen was finding it harder and harder to maintain a civil composure in the face of his stepmother's provocation.

Earlier this week he had reached his limit. He had come down one morning only to find that Caroline had preceded him and was waiting for him in the breakfast room. Her early rising was out of character, but it seemed she had been impatient to confront him. Only the night before she had learned of Miss Somerville's previous connection with her son, George.

Rather than being scandalized by George's behavior, Caroline professed herself vastly entertained. She praised Stephen for being willing to accept his brother's castoffs, but suggested that due to her experience, Miss Somerville was far better suited for the position of mistress rather than wife.

Stephen had blinked, seeing red. It had taken all of his self-control not to give in to the urge to slap the supercilious smile off Caroline's face. Instead, he had grimly informed her that this topic was never to be spoken of again. Ever. Or Lady Endicott would find herself banished to the dower house in the country.

Even Caroline seemed to realize that she had finally gone too far, for later that day she had begged his pardon and promised that she would treat Miss Somerville and her family with due respect and was looking forward to making their acquaintance. But he knew better than to trust the sincerity of her repentance. It would be best if she and the Somervilles had as little contact as possible.

A nudge on his arm roused him from his dark musings, and he heard the sound of thunderous applause. Miss Somerville rose to her feet, her gloved hands clapping, and Stephen rose to his own feet as well.

"Was that not absolutely marvelous? Sir Henry Richman is such a gifted speaker. He made me feel as if I had been to the Amazon myself," Miss Somerville declared.

"He has a way with words," Stephen agreed.

Miss Somerville was positively beaming with happiness, and Stephen wondered what he would have to do to make her look at him in such a way.

"Would you like to meet him?" he asked.

"Can we?"

"Of course," he said. There were some privileges to being a viscount, after all.

He waited until the crowds had thinned a little, then took Miss Somerville's arm and led her to the front of the hall. There Sir Henry Richman stood, surrounded on all sides by his enthralled admirers. At his side was Mr. Adam Baldwin, the secretary of the Explorers' Society. Stephen caught Mr. Baldwin's eye, and Mr. Baldwin nodded in recognition.

"Sir Henry, if I may," Mr. Baldwin said, as Sir Henry paused to take a breath. "There is a gentleman here you should meet."

The crowd parted, making room for him and Miss Somerville to approach.

"This is Viscount Endicott, a member of the Explorers' Society and a patron of your expedition to Brazil," Mr. Baldwin said.

Sir Henry smiled broadly. "Lord Endicott, I am at your service. Indeed, I am in your debt, for without benefactors such as yourself, my great explorations would still be but a dream."

"Sir Henry," Stephen said neutrally. "And may I present my fiancée, Miss Diana Somerville? She is a great admirer of yours."

Sir Henry gave a small bow. "I am honored."

"The honor is mine," Miss Somerville said. "The viscount was kind enough to give me a copy of your book, and ever since reading it, I have been longing to meet such an intrepid adventurer."

Sir Henry rocked back on his heels, his chest puffing out in self-congratulation. "It was nothing," he said, with false modesty. "Indeed, I am certain any Englishman would have done as well in my place."

Of that Stephen had little doubt. A trained monkey might have done as much.

"Or Englishwoman perhaps?" Miss Somerville prompted. "In these enlightened times, would not a female be just as suited for explorations?"

"No, no," Sir Henry said, and there were mutters of agreement from the gentlemen who surrounded him. "A female is too delicate to undertake such a journey. And to deliberately expose yourself to such dangers, not to mention the uncouth natives, is sheer folly."

"But Lady Hester Stanhope—"

"Is hardly a model we would wish our wives or daughters to follow. Is that not right, Lord Endicott?"

At least now the gentleman was talking sense. And Miss Somerville was glaring daggers at Sir Henry, which perversely made Stephen feel more in charity with the gentleman.

"I know the life of an explorer carries risk, and the families they leave behind must worry about them. It is only natural to wish that those we love remain safe," Lord Endicott said diplomatically. He sensed Miss Somerville was prepared to stay and argue her case, and he moved swiftly to forestall the inevitable scene.

"Come now, Miss Somerville, we must not monopolize the gentleman's time. Sir Henry, Mr. Baldwin," he said, with a nod of his head in dismissal.

Miss Somerville was still fuming as they stood on the steps waiting for a hackney coach to arrive.

"For such a great explorer, Sir Henry has a very limited view of the world," Miss Somerville said. "He was entirely too quick to dismiss the idea of female explorers."

Stephen said nothing, hoping she would change the topic. But Miss Somerville was nothing if not persistent.

"And you, my lord, what do you think? Do you think women should be allowed to take their place in the world? Or are adventures the sole province of the male sex?"

Stephen looked at her, knowing she would not be put off by half-truths. "I do not think women are fit for the hardships of exploring. But in honesty, I do not think Sir Henry is much of an explorer either. I will wager the unfortunate Mr. Watkins did the real work. His death was the real reason why Sir Henry turned back. It was not out of grief for the loss of his companion, but because he was too chicken-hearted to go on alone."

Miss Somerville glared at him, and then her face relaxed in a smile. "You are too cynical for your own good, my lord," she said.

"And you are too innocent," he said. And far too trusting to be allowed out in the world on her own, where others would be certain to take advantage of her.

"Then, we make a fine pair, indeed," she said.

That night, Diana dreamed that she was with Sir Henry Richman's party as they began the exploration of the Amazon. They sailed up the broad river, deeper and deeper into the dense green jungle, leaving civilization far behind. And when they were attacked by hostile natives, and Sir Henry wounded, it was she who rallied the party and held them together until they could make their escape. Her companions were lavish in their praise for her cool-headedness, but when she turned to receive the approbation of the expedition leader, she found Lord Endicott had taken the place of Sir Henry.

A most odd dream, indeed, she mused, for her waking mind knew how improbable it was that someone as conservative as Lord Endicott would ever leave the comforts of civilization to embark upon the hazardous life of an explorer. Perhaps she had dreamt of him because he was a friend. Or perhaps because she had found Sir Henry to be a bit of a disappointment, with his old-fashioned views on the capabilities of the female sex. One would have thought that an explorer would be more openminded about such things. Still, there was no denying that Sir Henry, despite his own shortcomings, was an inspiration to her, and she longed for the day that she could set off upon her own adventures.

Perhaps she was wrong to think of exploring Brazil. No doubt other explorers were already following in the path that Sir Henry had blazed. It might be better to start somewhere fresh, to blaze her own trail. Egypt, for example. The ancient land of the Pharaohs held its own exotic secrets, and only the lower part of the Nile River had been traversed by Europeans. Who knew what wonders she might find if she journeyed along the length of the Nile to find its legendary source?

"What do you think, dear?"

"The Nile," Diana replied. "But I must seek out books on their native tongue, and perhaps I can find an instructor who is willing to tutor me in Arabic."

"What on earth are you talking about?" her mother asked.

Diana blinked and looked around. She was not sailing on a barge along the Nile, nor was she in her own sitting room. Instead, she was in the back room of the mantua maker's, surrounded by bolts of fabrics and open pattern books.

Her mother sat on a small chair across from her, and her face bore the expression of one long resigned to her daughter's follies.

"I am sorry, Mama. I was woolgathering," Diana apologized.

"Evidently."

Mrs. Somerville gestured toward the open pattern book and picked up one of the fabric swatches in her hand, rubbing it between her fingers.

"So, which fabric do you prefer? The figured muslin is nice and could be trimmed in red to match the flowers. Or there is the French washing silk. It is quite elegant, but I do not know if such a fabric is sturdy enough for a walking dress. Perhaps in London, but it would certainly never do for a country outing."

Diana shrugged. She had little interest in clothing and did not understand why her mother felt compelled to order these new gowns for her. It had been tedious enough enduring the fittings back in the winter, when she had been preparing for the season. But now, merely because she was engaged to a viscount, her mother seemed to think that an entirely new wardrobe was required. And nothing Diana said had any effect upon her mother's determination to see that Diana was displayed to her best advantage.

"The figured muslin," Diana said, after a long pause. "If the dress does not suit me, I know it will become Mary nicely."

"Mary will have her own dresses made when it is her time," her mother said. "Today we are discussing your wardrobe."

Which was a shame, really, for both their sakes. Mary enjoyed discussing fashions, and she loved nothing better than pouring through the latest fashion plates. If Mary were here, she would be in her element.

Unlike Diana, who thought longingly of making her escape.

"I see no reason to order so many new frocks," Diana said. "The new ball gown I understand, but, as for the rest, once I return to Kent, I will have no use for them."

"A viscountess must be fashionably dressed," her mother said.

Diana glanced around.

"Yes, but I am not to be a viscountess," Diana said, keeping her voice soft. The mantua maker had disappeared upstairs to fetch more samples of her work, but there was no telling when she would return. "When the summer is over, we will put this folly behind us, and I will have no use for fine dresses when I am off upon my adventures."

Mrs. Somerville shuddered and made a moue of distaste. "Do not speak of such things," she said. "I cannot bear to think of a daughter of mine off wandering in such distant lands. I am hoping you come to your senses and see the folly of your course."

"I know my own mind," Diana said.

Her mother seemed prepared to argue her point, but just then Mrs. Baker appeared, carrying a silk ball gown in her arms, trailed by her assistant, who held a half dozen fabric bolts stacked in her arms.

Her mother exclaimed over the beautiful gown, and Diana welcomed the distraction it provided. She had no wish to quarrel with her mother. It was still some years before she would be free to make her way in the world. Ample time for her mother to resign herself to the knowledge that her eldest daughter was too unconventional to accept the restrictions of a society marriage. In the meantime, if it made her mother happy to lavish a few gowns upon her, then it would be churlish of Diana to refuse her that pleasure.

Eight

Light spilled forth from the windows of the Grosvenor Square mansion, illuminating the soft June night. A small crowd of onlookers watched as a procession of private carriages and hackney coaches drew up in front of the steps, and liveried footmen helped the elegantly dressed passengers alight.

Inside, the great house shone as it had not done in years, as guests circulated among the festively decorated public rooms. The dowager Lady Endicott had outdone herself. In the ballroom, a fashionable orchestra played as guests danced underneath fairy lights and hanging silk ribbons. Gentlemen played cards in the library, while in the Chinese parlor ladies fatigued from the dancing could rest on couches and gossip decorously. And in the dining room, where a full forty guests had sat down for dinner, extra servants hired for this evening now arranged a lavish buffet to be served at midnight.

This ball would be the talk of the season, and Stephen knew he owed Caroline his thanks. Indeed, he had much to be grateful for, he reflected, as he accepted the congratulations of yet another well-wisher.

He entered the ballroom, moving around the edges of the crowd until he spotted Diana's black hair among the myriad of couples dancing. Her height made her easy to find; in fact, she towered over her unfortunate partner. But she did not seem to mind.

Stephen stood, taking pleasure in watching her enjoyment. It was a shame that the rules of propriety were so strict. They had opened the dance together, as was fitting. But he would not be allowed to claim his second dance until much later in the evening.

He wondered what gossips would say if he dared to claim a third dance. No doubt it would be taken as a sign of his infatuation. From the remarks he had overheard this evening, the whole of London believed this to be a love match and thought him to be hopelessly besotted with his betrothed. Speculation about Miss Somerville's feelings was less clear. Some thought her equally in love, while others credited her with cool calculation and taking advantage of the viscount's infatuation.

It should have cheered him to know that their deception had worked so well. It was what they had hoped for when entering into this engagement. But, instead, such thoughts were oddly depressing. The more folk congratulated him on his good fortune, the lower his mood became.

It was not real, he reminded himself, as he gazed at Diana. This was not real. She was not his. This was only a play, and at the end, they would go their separate ways.

But did they really have to part? He had grown fond of Diana in these past weeks, and he thought she was fond of him as well. As a friend and companion, at least. Perhaps by the time they reached the autumn, they would realize that they no longer wished to part. Perhaps she would agree to become his wife in truth.

Or perhaps she would cheerfully bid him farewell and think no more of him as she made her plans to venture off to India or South America or whatever uncharted wilderness attracted her fantasy. In a few years he might hear of her exploits, recounted in some newspaper.

"You look uncommonly grim for a gentleman celebrating his engagement."

Stephen turned and saw Tony Dunne had come up to stand beside him. He forced himself to smile.

"Just woolgathering," he said. "I think this is going very well, do you not?"

Tony Dunne looked around at the packed ballroom, filled with the cream of London society come to celebrate his friend's engagement. "Certainly the ball is a success. But are you having regrets about the other?"

There was no need for him to elaborate. As the weeks had passed, and Stephen had spent more and more time in Miss Somerville's company, Tony Dunne had become increasingly concerned for his friend. He had warned Stephen more than once that it was foolish to become so attached to a woman who planned to walk away from this engagement wholehearted.

"Not regrets. Not precisely," Stephen said softly, so that no one could overhear him. "Rather I am thinking about opportunities."

Tony Dunne raised one eyebrow. "Considering how well Miss Somerville would fit the role of Lady Endicott?"

He knew Diana would do very well as Lady Endicott. Once he convinced her to give over her foolish notions of exploring the uncharted corners of the world. But even then, would she agree to have him? Or would she want a gentleman who shared her taste for the unconventional?

"I am thinking it is past time I followed your example and found a wife to settle down with," Stephen said.

"Stephen," Tony began.

"Do not say it," Stephen interrupted him. He did not want to hear another lecture on caution or on how fundamentally unsuited he and Miss Somerville were. Tonight was theirs, and he planned to enjoy himself. There would be time enough for caution and regrets on the morrow.

"Trust me, I know what I am doing," he said.

As the country dance drew to a close, Diana Somerville gave a sigh of relief. Mr. Hopkins was pleasant enough, but not only was he so short that she looked down upon his balding pate, but the unfortunate gentleman lacked all sense of direction or rhythm. Time and time again, she and the other dancers in their set had had to gently steer him in the right direction. Once, when changing partners, he had blundered into another set entirely. It had taken several measures for him to realize his mistake.

"A very great pleasure, Miss Somerville," Mr. Hopkins said, withdrawing a handkerchief and mopping his brow.

"I thank you," Diana said, with a practiced smile. It could have been worse, she reflected. She and Mr. Hopkins could have been dancing a waltz.

But there were only two waltzes planned, and Lord Endicott had boldly claimed them for himself. Not that Diana was in any mood to disagree. Indeed, it was pleasant to have such a companionable partner.

Mr. Hopkins led her back to the sidelines, where her mother sat chatting with her friends. Their hostess, the dowager Lady Endicott, had disappeared some time before. No doubt she was supervising the servants, ensuring that the guests in the other rooms were comfortable and that all was in readiness for the midnight supper.

As Diana waited for her next partner to claim her, she caught sight of Lord Endicott, who stood across the room, in conversation with his friend Mr. Dunne. Sensing himself under observation, Lord Endicott looked up and then smiled as she caught his eye.

Diana smiled and inclined her head in recognition. She wished suddenly that he was her next partner. She wanted to tell him how much she was enjoying herself. Tonight was absolutely perfect; between them, he and his stepmother had outdone themselves. Their engagement ball was already being called the event of the season. It was what every young woman dreamed of.

But it was only a pretense, she reminded herself. She and the viscount were but characters in a play, performing for their audience. And yet it was harder and harder to remember that they were only playing their roles and that they were not in truth two people in love, who intended to be married and to spend the rest of their lives together.

Diana frowned and turned slightly, gazing at her mother. Mrs. Somerville had been the first to fall into the trap, she realized. For weeks now her mother had been referring to Diana's marriage as if it were an accepted fact. "When you are married," she would say, and Diana, mindful of the listening servants, hesitated to correct her.

She, too, was to blame, for Diana had indulged in her own share of foolish daydreams. It was simply that she was not an actress. She was not used to pretending, and certainly not for carrying out a deception for more than a month. With all those around her constantly referring to the fact of her impending marriage, and treating Lord Endicott as her fiancé, it was no wonder that Diana, herself, occasionally lost sight of the truth.

When Lord Endicott had first proposed his plan, it had all seemed so simple. They would announce their engagement and then appear in society a handful of times to prove that they were, indeed, a couple. Then they would go their separate ways, until the autumn when they would announce that she had chosen to break off the engagement.

But rather than seeing Lord Endicott a mere handful of times, she saw him almost every day. She had come to rely upon his steady and undemanding presence. When a day or two passed where she did not see him, she found herself oddly at loose ends, as if she were somehow not complete without him.

She realized she had become dangerously dependent upon the viscount's friendship. And such was folly, for it would only make it harder for them to part when the time came. Diana realized that she must be more cautious in the future. After tonight, there would be no question in society's mind of the truth of their engagement. There would be no need for her and Lord Endicott to be constantly in each other's company, and a cooling off period would give them both time to reflect and to regain their equilibrium. And then, at the end of June, she could return to the country and take up the threads of her old life. No doubt Lord Endicott was equally anxious to resume his own well-ordered existence, without the demands of catering to a fiancée.

Her musings were interrupted by the appearance of a young gentleman, who bowed before her. "I apologize for being late, but I believe this is my dance," he said.

She recalled him only vaguely. His name was Fawkes or Ffolkes or some such, but she did, indeed, remember promising him a dance. So Diana allowed him to take her hand and lead her out to join a set of latecomers that was just forming.

The musicians were playing a quadrille, a slow, stately dance that allowed the partners much time for leisured conversation.

Her partner was a slightly built gentleman, close to herself in age. There was something about him that seemed vaguely familiar.

"I am sorry, I do not recall your name," Diana said.

"Fox. Mr. Arthur Fox," her partner said.

"Of course," Diana said. And, indeed, the name rang a bell in her mind. But she could not place it.

"May I offer my felicitations upon your engagement?"

"Thank you," Diana replied, as she had a score or more times already this evening.

Mr. Fox fell silent, allowing Diana to concentrate on the figures of the dance, while around them the three other couples were busy flirting, engaged in lively conversation. In the set opposite hers, Diana caught sight of Lord Endicott, partnered with Elizabeth Dunne.

Mr. Fox followed the direction of her gaze. "I was surprised to hear of your engagement," he said.

Diana raised one eyebrow haughtily. "Indeed?"

"You may not recall, but we had met before. In April. George introduced us."

For a brief moment her steps faltered as she recalled that Mr. Fox was one of the set of young wastrels who had surrounded George that spring. Then she regained her footing, and her mental equilibrium. There was no point in letting Mr. Fox know that he had discomfited her.

"I have been so busy of late, I can scarcely recall those days. They seem like ancient history," she said, striving for lightness. She hoped Mr. Fox would heed the warning in her words.

Mr. Fox licked his lips, then glanced around nervously. "I do not mean to bring back unpleasant memories," he said. "I just wanted to say that I wish you well. Truly. I think Lord Endicott is a fine gentleman," he said.

His eyes beseeched her, and Diana realized that he had not meant to embarrass her. Rather, this young cub was asking for her forgiveness, though he could scarcely have chosen a worse time or place. Had he no sense of discretion?

"There we can agree," Diana said. "Lord Endicott may appear reserved, but once you get to know him, you realize that he is worth a dozen of his brother. One could do worse than follow his example."

"So I have learned," Mr. Fox said.

Diana waited until a few measures had passed before asking, "Tell me, what do you hear from Mr. Wright these days?"

Mr. Fox shook his head. "I have heard nothing," he said. "And I do not expect to, for I have broken off that connection."

"That is for the best," Diana said.

Such was her good humor this evening that she was inclined to forgive Mr. Fox for whatever part he had played in that disastrous affair. He was only a boy, really. There was still time for him to mend his ways, now that he was free from George's influence.

"Tell me, what do you think of the news from the Continent? Will Napoleon turn tail? Or will Wellington finally be able to face him on the field of battle?" Diana asked.

Mr. Fox accepted the change of subject gratefully, and they ended the dance in charity with each other.

As befitted his duties as host, Stephen danced several dances with ladies of his acquaintance, but a part of his attention was always on Miss Somerville. She seemed to be enjoying herself immensely, as were their guests. Even he, who normally loathed such crowded events, had to admit that he was enjoying tonight's festivities.

He had been concerned when he saw Diana partnered with George's crony, Mr. Fox. A part of him wanted to tear them apart and to rip a strip off that young gentleman's hide for having the impertinence to dare approach Diana. But his wiser self had prevailed, seeing that Diana did not appear in the least distressed.

Still, he inwardly railed against the conventions that strictly limited the attentions that he could pay Miss Somerville, even at a ball held in their honor.

After making certain that Mr. Fox relinquished Miss Somerville to her next partner without incident, Stephen made his excuses and went to check on the gentlemen who had taken themselves off to the card room. He stayed there only briefly, resisting the urgings of one of his friends to take part in a friendly hand of cards, and then, as soon as politeness permitted, he made his return to the ballroom.

As midnight approached, he found himself growing more restless. He was relieved when the conductor finally announced that the next dance would be the supper dance. With quick steps he navigated the ballroom, to where Diana's last partner stood talking to her. One brief look was enough to send Mr. Campbell on his way, and then he had her to himself.

"Have I told you how lovely you look this evening?" he asked.

"At least twice." Diana laughed.

Just seeing her, standing here talking to her, was enough to lighten his spirits. Even to inspire him to levity, as if he were once again a green boy.

"Well, then, I have been terribly remiss. I meant to tell you at least thrice," he said. "Miss Somerville, I vow that you are the prettiest lady in all of London this evening."

"Only in London?"

"My mistake. In all of England," he said, pressing his right hand over his heart to indicate his sincerity.

"And I will even proclaim you to be far prettier than the ladies of Brazil and the Indian continent."

Miss Somerville's blue eyes twinkled. "Flatterer."

"I speak only the truth," he said. "For I have eyes for no one but you."

As he said the words, he realized that they were, indeed, true. Tony Dunne had been right to be concerned. Stephen had long ago forgotten that he was only pretending. In these past weeks, he had played the part of doting fiancé so well that he was no longer certain where the role ended and he began. He realized that he no longer cared. It did not matter that he had entered into this engagement out of a sense of duty or that he and Miss Somerville were almost completely unsuited for each other in temperament and philosophy.

When he was with her he was happy. It was that simple. Even knowing that Miss Somerville was undoubtedly playacting as well did not dampen his enthusiasm. She liked him. He was certain of that much. And, given time, he could convince her to make this a real engagement and to marry him in truth.

"Come now, they are waiting for us," Miss Somerville prompted him.

"Of course," he said, and he led her into the center of the ballroom as the orchestra struck up a waltz tune.

The daring waltz allowed him an intimacy that was nearly a public embrace, with one hand resting on Miss Somerville's trim waist, while the other clasped her hand to his. And unlike most women, her height meant he could look her in the face and catch every nuance of her expression. They fit well together, he decided, and not just on the dance floor.

"You are enjoying yourself?" he asked.

"Immensely," Miss Somerville replied. "I have never before had a ball held in my honor, and I recommend the experience highly. I wished to thank Lady Endicott for making this such a wonderful occasion, but I have not seen her in some time."

Stephen glanced around, but his stepmother's plumed headdress was nowhere to be seen. Strange. Caroline had been called away earlier by one of the servants, but whatever domestic crisis had prompted her to leave should have been solved by now. And it was not like her to miss any opportunity to reign over a ballroom.

"Perhaps she is overseeing the arrangements in the supper room," he said.

Miss Somerville nodded. "Of course, I should have thought of that. It is just that I have seen so little of her this evening. I had hoped to have a chance to become acquainted with her."

The less time Miss Somerville spent with Caroline, the better, in his opinion, but he knew better than to voice such a thought aloud. He and Miss Somerville had already quarreled once over his stepmother. He did not intend to repeat that quarrel tonight.

"The demands on a hostess are many," he said placatingly. "No doubt there will be other occasions in the future where you both will be able to converse at leisure."

If they were, indeed, to be married in truth, then Diana and Caroline would have to come to an understanding. Much as he would like to deny the connection, unless his stepmother chose to remarry, she would perforce be a part of his life. A distant part, to be certain, but nonetheless present.

"Your father seemed quite contented in the card room," Stephen said. "And your mother seems pleased with the festivities. If she has told me once how happy she is, she has told me a half dozen times."

"Mama is in high alt. Indeed, I quite think she has forgotten the bargain we made," Miss Somerville said. There was a pause as she looked downward at her feet and bit her lower lip with her pearl white teeth. "Sometimes I find myself forgetting that this is not real," she confessed.

His heart quickened, and he squeezed her hand in his. This was the opportunity he had been seeking. "About that—" he began.

He felt a tap on his shoulder, and he turned and then stopped still in frozen horror. Miss Somerville stepped on his foot and then clutched his arm to right herself at the sudden stop.

A part of his mind noticed that around them heads were turning, and the other couples were gradually coming to a halt as the inanely cheerful music continued on. But the rest of his attention was fixed on the man who stood before him.

"Dear brother, Miss Somerville," George Wright said, with a mocking gleam in his eye. "Forgive my tardiness, but I had to come and offer my congratulations."

"George," he said. And then his mind blanked, and he could think of nothing else to say. He was all too conscious of Miss Somerville, who was trembling with fury by his side, and the hundred pairs of eyes that were watching this family reunion with avid fascination. The last strains of the waltz faded away, ensuring that whatever they said would be overheard.

"I am so pleased to see that you have tended to my affairs," George said, his gaze insolently raking over Miss Somerville's body. "Your brotherly concern overwhelms me."

Stephen stepped in front of Miss Somerville, blocking her from his brother's gaze. He no longer cared that they had an audience. He would not permit anyone to insult his fiancée.

"Stephen," Diana said, resting her hand upon his forearm.

A silver bell rang, and heads turned to the main doors, which had been thrown open.

"Ladies and gentlemen, please join me in the supper room," Lady Endicott said, and as she nodded, two footmen threw open the doors that connected the ballroom to the dining room.

Even the hope of witnessing a scandal was not enough to distract the guests from the prospect of a lavish buffet, and couples began to stream through the double doors.

"This is not over," Stephen warned his half brother.

"I did not think it was," George replied. "Miss Somerville, I look forward to renewing our acquaintance."

Then, with one last mocking glance, George disappeared, leaving Stephen to escort a white-faced Miss Somerville into the supper room, where they attempted to appear as if nothing were at all amiss.

Nine

The sight of his brother provoked a murderous rage within Stephen. It took every ounce of his self-control not to give in to the urge to plant the facer that George so richly deserved. Instead, drawing upon acting skills honed over these past weeks, Stephen managed to greet his brother with at least the appearance of civility. The pretense may have fooled others, but he knew from his brother's mocking gaze that George, at least, knew full well how much Stephen loathed him.

Miss Somerville, for her part, managed to play her role to perfection, accepting George's felicitations with good grace. And when the cur had the temerity to take a seat by them at the supper table, Diana even condescended to address a few questions to him, inquiring about his travels. Stephen could only imagine how much the effort cost her. Here she was, forced to make polite conversation with the man who had conspired to ruin her.

He was heartily relieved when Tony and Elizabeth Dunne joined them at the small table, taking upon themselves the burden of the conversation. He counted himself blessed to have them as friends. But even as he pretended to eat the sawdust on the plate before him,

he found himself battling his conflicting impulses as
his anger warred with his intellect.

He wanted to throw George out on the street. He
wanted to take Diana from this place and keep her safe
from all those who would harm her. And yet he could
do no such thing. He knew that George's sudden return
was on everyone's lips, and the three of them were the
center of attention. The gossips would seize upon any
sign of discord or public display of distress. It would
take only a moment to destroy all the work they had
done in these past weeks to restore Diana's reputation.

For himself he did not care. He was willing to tell
the whole world to go hang, rather than to endure one
more minute of his brother's perfidy. But for Diana's
sake he gritted his teeth and behaved himself with the
appearance of civility.

It seemed an eternity before the supper was over and
the guests began to take their leave. He was not surprised when Mr. Somerville was among the first to
announce his intention to depart, claiming his daughter
was fatigued from the excitement of the evening. It
was only the simple truth, after all.

Stephen escorted them to the door and stood with
them as their carriage was summoned.

"I am more sorry than I can say," he told her, and
as he said the words, he flashed back upon their first
meeting. It seemed all he did was apologize to her for
the hurt his brother had caused her. "I admire your
courage. You did very well tonight," he added.

Diana squeezed his hand. "It is done now," she said
cryptically. Her gaze was focused straight ahead, and
she would not meet his eyes.

"I will see you tomorrow," he said, loudly enough for her parents to overhear.

"Diana will be quite busy tomorrow, entertaining callers come to pay their respects," Mrs. Somerville said. She, at least, seemed oblivious to the tension that swirled around the others.

Damn. He had forgotten about that. Custom dictated that those gentlemen who had danced with Diana tonight call upon her on the morrow, to express their appreciation. And, of course, there would no doubt be both well-wishers and curiosity seekers who wished to talk to her about the events of this evening.

"I will see you in the morning, then," he said. He had no mind to sit in a drawing room surrounded by other callers and make polite conversation. He had to see her. Alone.

Just then he heard the sound of the church bells striking the hour of one.

Diana turned to face him at last, a rueful smile on her lips. "It is already morning," she said.

"Then, I will see you later this morning," he said.

She nodded, and with that he had to be content.

The hired carriage drew up in front of the steps, and the footman helped her parents ascend. Stephen helped Diana in himself, wrapping the carriage blanket tightly around her. He knew he must look like a besotted fool, but at the moment he did not care.

"It will be all right," Diana said gravely.

Strange, that she should be reassuring him.

"I will make it so," he vowed.

And then, reluctantly, he stepped back and watched

as the footman closed the carriage door, and the coach drove off into the night.

Returning indoors, he had cause to regret his stepmother's lavish hospitality. Some of the guests were enjoying themselves too much to leave, despite the departure of the guests of honor. When subtle hints did not work, Stephen resorted to blunt statements that it was time to leave. When even that proved ineffective, Stephen ordered the footmen to begin dousing the lamps. At this, the last dozen or so hangers-on remaining finally departed, expressing their astonishment at the lateness of the hour.

It was past three o'clock in the morning when the last inebriated guest was finally poured down the stairs and into a hackney coach. Stephen watched his departure with a frown, then went in search of his family.

He found Caroline and her son, George, in the Chinese parlor. Caroline was reclining on a sofa while George lounged in a chair, a brandy bottle at his elbow.

Stephen wasted no time. "I want you gone," he said flatly.

"But I have only just arrived," George replied.

"Then, you have no need to unpack your bags," Stephen said. "I want you gone. From this house, from London, from England. I do not want to see your face until after my marriage, do you understand?"

He did not know when he had decided that he was no longer playing the part of a fiancé and that he wanted Diana to be his wife. It had come on him gradually, seeping into his consciousness slowly over the course of these weeks. But he knew it now for the truth. He had known it even before George made his untimely appearance. But now, with George here, it made it all the more urgent that Stephen and Diana be wed. The sooner, the better.

He wondered if he could convince her to have the first banns read this Sunday. They could be married in just three weeks if she agreed.

"No," George said.

"Stephen, there is no need to bully poor George in this unseemly fashion," Caroline said. "At least hear what he has to say."

Stephen sighed and then took a seat in a stiff-backed chair across from the other two.

"I am listening."

"I know what I did was wrong. It was a foolish prank done in drunken folly," George said. He gave a rueful smile, as if confessing to a small boy's mischief. "It did not take me long to regret what I had done."

"So you left the country," Stephen said.

"My friends and I had long planned the journey. I went with them because I could not see what else to do. But as time passed, I came to realize the consequences of what I had done. I could not live with myself, so I came back to London to make my apologies," George said. "Imagine my surprise when I arrived here to find a party in progress, and my shock when I learned the reason for the celebration."

It was a plausible tale, but Stephen had learned through bitter experience that he could not trust his brother's words. George was equally comfortable bending the truth or lying outright. And he was at his most dangerous when he appeared to be sincere.

"And you decided that having arrived, you had nothing better to do than to make a dramatic appearance? Why not stay out of sight until you could speak to me privately?"

George shrugged. "I had no reason to keep my arrival secret. Several of your late-arriving guests were in the foyer when I made my entrance. Since they knew I was here, it seemed foolish to skulk in my room."

"And did you not once think of how I would feel? How Miss Somerville would feel, when confronted by you so unexpectedly? You could at least have sent a servant with a message, warning us."

"George does not think like you. He is not naturally cold and suspicious. He thought you would be pleased to see him," Lady Endicott said, defending her son.

Stephen raised his hands and slowly began to massage his temples. He could feel a monster headache forming, brought on by weariness and the strain of the evening. His earlier anger had been replaced by a dull fury and the certain knowledge that he could not give in to his cravings. One did not call out one's own brother, no matter how reprehensible his conduct may have been.

"So tell me, why are you really here?" he asked, more out of habit than out of any expectation of receiving the truth.

"I came to make amends," George said. "But I see you have already done that, and far surpassed any puny efforts I might make on my own behalf."

"Fine. So now you will leave." Stephen did not really believe that George had returned to make his apologies. There was some other motive here. Something that in his anger and tiredness he was not seeing. Perhaps it was simply that George had become bored upon the Continent or that he had run short of funds and returned to his doting mama. But a part of Stephen discounted such easy explanations. There was more afoot here than met the eye.

"It took me over a week to get here," George said. "Now that I am back in London, I have a mind to stay and enjoy the remainder of the season. Surely you can have no reason to object."

"I have every reason to object. You have caused enough scandal for one season. I have no mind to bear witness to your next disaster, nor will I stand idly by while you hurt another innocent."

"I am a changed man," George said, his face solemn. If one did not know him, one might suspect that he was actually contrite. But Stephen knew better.

"Then, I will do as I must," Stephen said, thinking aloud. "Stay in London, if you are determined to do so, but I can and will forbid you this house. You are not welcome here, not as long as I remain in residence."

"You cannot do this," Lady Endicott protested. "This is my house, and I will have as I please under my roof."

Stephen rose. "We have already had this conversation, madame," he said, a chill in his voice. "You may stay here as long as you abide by my rules. Or do you truly wish to remove yourself to the dower house at Eastbourne?"

Caroline made no reply.

"I thought as much," he said. "Then, I suggest you bid good night to your son here. He is leaving."

"Stephen, be reasonable; it is nearly dawn. What would it hurt if he stayed here tonight?" Caroline said.

George made no comment in his own defense, relying upon his mother to soften Stephen's harsh judgment. It was a strategy that had worked in the past, but did so no longer.

"Your concern for your son is touching, if misplaced. You should save your pity for those he has harmed. If I were you, I would do my best to rein him in. I warn you both, my patience is at an end. And you do not want to make me into an enemy."

As the carriage drew away from Grosvenor Square, Mrs. Somerville reached across the seats and patted her daughter on the hand. "You did very well tonight, Diana. No young lady there could hold a candle to you, in beauty or in grace. Even that old stickler Lady Wharton condescended to praise you, saying that you were born to be a viscountess."

Mrs. Somerville beamed at her daughter in a rare show of approval. It was a marked contrast from Diana's first sojourn in London, when after each society affair her mother would gaze at her reproachfully and urge Diana to follow the example of the other young ladies of the *ton*. Diana had protested in vain that she had no wish to be thought a witless sheep, but her mother had persisted in her belief that for Diana to be truly happy she must conform to the role that society had assigned to her.

And now, apparently, her earlier stubbornness was forgiven. Mrs. Somerville was basking in the glow of having successfully fired off her eldest daughter, securing a viscount, no less. Diana stared at her mother with incomprehension. How could her mother have forgotten so quickly that the engagement was a sham, meant to hide a scandal? She loved her mother, but she did not understand her. And she suspected that her mother felt the same mixture of affection and bafflement whenever she was confronted with her eldest daughter.

"Awkward bit, there," her father said. "Mr. Wright, returning as he did."

Awkward was such a tepid word. It had been a shock. An insult. A cruel blow to her composure.

"It was a surprise," Diana said, choosing her words with care. If he sensed her distress, her father would insist on talking about what had happened. And she was too tired, and her nerves too raw, for such a conversation. "I suppose it was inevitable that we would encounter one another at some point. At least now that unpleasantness is over with."

Her father looked at her searchingly, and then with a faint shrug of his shoulders, he seemed prepared to let the subject drop. For that mercy she was thankful.

For the remainder of the drive she sat in silence, having only to murmur the occasional word of assent, as her mother continued to chatter on about the ball and Lady Endicott's lavish hospitality.

Mrs. Somerville seemed prepared to talk until the dawn, but as soon as they reached the town house, Diana made her escape, pleading fatigue, and retired to her chambers.

She found her maid, Jenna, dozing on a cot in the dressing room, and with her help removed the elaborate ball gown and then donned her cambric night rail.

She dismissed her maid and crawled into bed, but she knew that she would not sleep.

Her mind was racing in all directions, and her emotions were equally unsettled. She wished desperately for someone to talk to, someone who would understand her feelings. But the only one she could think of was Lord Endicott, and it would be hours before she would see him again.

She knew she should be angry, even outraged that George Wright had dared to attend the ball. Even his mere presence in London would have been distasteful, but nothing could compare to his effrontery in appearing at a ball meant to celebrate her engagement to his brother. An engagement that would not have been necessary had George Wright behaved with even a shred of decency.

A part of her felt anger, while another part wondered at the reasons for his return. Why had he come to London? And why had he chosen this night, of all nights, to make his appearance? Had it simply been ill luck?

But mixed with her anger was another emotion. It took her a while to recognize it as disbelief. For nearly two months now she had cast George Wright in the role of a villain, one who had tried his best to ruin her. A man who had proven himself without honor or decency. A monster. And yet as her initial shock had worn off, her anger had turned to a kind of amazement. George Wright was a villainous cad, that was true. But now she saw what she had not seen before. George Wright was a callow young man, barely more than a boy for all his veneer of sophistication. The contrast between him and his brother could not have been greater.

It was hard to believe that she had once thought George Wright charming. If she had met him tonight for the first time, she would not have given him a second glance.

Then again, before now her standards of comparison had been rather limited. There had been few young gentlemen in her neighborhood at home, and none whom she would have called friend. Now, she was wiser. Her acquaintance with Lord Endicott had shown her the true measure of a gentleman, and George Wright fell far short of that standard.

As he had promised, Lord Endicott called upon her the next morning, at the barely civilized hour of nine o'clock. Diana was still in the breakfast room, having arisen only shortly before.

"Please join me," she said, and Lord Endicott took the empty seat to her left. "Will you have tea? Chocolate? Coffee?"

"Coffee would be pleasant," Lord Endicott replied.

She dispatched a footman for the coffee and used the opportunity to study the viscount. His shadowed eyes and drawn face told her that he, too, had passed a sleepless night. She wondered what conclusions he drew from her own pale face and the dark smudges under her eyes.

The servant set a china cup of coffee in front of Lord Endicott. "Will you be joining Miss Somerville for breakfast, my lord? Cook would be pleased to make a plate for you."

"No, just the coffee is fine. Thank you, Daniels," Lord Endicott said. He gave a nod, and the footman departed, closing the door behind him.

"We can talk freely," Diana said. "After last night's excitement, my parents are unlikely to stir before noon."

Lord Endicott busied himself by pouring sugar in his coffee and then stirred it slowly with a spoon. "About last night," he began. "I swear to you that I had no idea that George was going to make an appearance. I thought him still safely on the Continent."

"Why did he come back?" Diana asked.

The viscount's eyes remained focused on the coffee in front of him, though he had yet to take a single sip. "I no longer try to fathom the motives behind anything that George does," Lord Endicott said bitterly. Then he raised his eyes to hers. "George claimed that he was unaware of our engagement. Said it was mere coincidence that he happened to arrive when he did."

"Do you believe him?"

Lord Endicott shrugged. "It does not matter why he came, only that he is here now. And he intends to stay."

The news gave Diana a cold feeling in her stomach. Through the long night she had consoled herself with the thought that somehow Lord Endicott would take charge and make her troubles magically disappear. She was convinced that he would be able to banish his brother from London. At least until after the season was over, and she and her parents returned to Kent.

But Lord Endicott was not invincible after all.

"Is he likely to cause trouble?" she asked.

"I have warned him of the seriousness of the situation and the dangers of crossing my will. Hopefully prudence will dictate his course. But I have taken the precaution of banning him from Grosvenor Square. And with his reputation, it is unlikely that he will be invited to the more select *ton* gatherings. With a little effort we can avoid encountering him."

It was an impossible tangle, and Diana took a sip of her chocolate as she thought through the implications of his statement. Would it really be that simple? Or was Lord Endicott fooling himself?

"And what will society say when they learn we will not accept invitations where Mr. Wright may be present? Indeed, what do you think they are saying after last night?" she asked.

"No doubt his sudden appearance will have caused a buzz, but our apparent cordiality should prevent anyone from trying to revive the old gossip," Lord Endicott said.

"So if we now begin to avoid him, people will begin to wonder why, and the whole ugly story will come out," Diana said. She was angry. These past weeks had been a wasted effort. If she was destined to be embroiled in scandal, she might as well have stayed in Kent. There, at least, she knew who she was.

"It seems to me we have little choice," she continued. "If we avoid your brother, we run the risk of fueling the very gossip we hope to avoid. And yet the alternative, that of seeking out your brother's company, is even more unbearable."

Last night had been torture enough. She had no wish to encounter George Wright again. Ever.

Lord Endicott pushed his coffee away and then reached over to take her hand in his. "There is another alternative," he said.

She raised one eyebrow. "And?"

"Marry me," he said. "We can post the first banns this weekend and be married in three week's time at St. George's. Once you are Lady Endicott, you will have nothing to fear. Not from my brother, nor from society gossip."

She withdrew her hand from his. "Are you mad?" she asked, in an echo of their first conversation. "Rushing into a hasty marriage may be exactly what your brother wants. Why would you let him dictate the course of the rest of your life?"

Perversely now her hand felt cold, and she wished he would retake it in his. But he did not.

"I did not think of it in that light," he said.

"And as for the gossip, I am thick-skinned enough to bear the scorn of a few malicious harpies. Can you say the same?"

"I was only thinking of protecting you," he said.

It was lowering to realize that he still thought of her in terms of duty and honor. As if she were a responsibility that had been entrusted to his care. Her own feelings toward him had changed, but apparently his had not.

"I appreciate your concern. But there is no need for us to take such hasty action," Diana replied.

"I will abide by your wishes," Lord Endicott said. "But should you change your mind—"

"I will not," Diana interrupted him. She would not marry for the sake of convenience, no matter how much she had come to value Lord Endicott's friendship.

It would be different if he had spoken of passion. If he urged this marriage not out of fear of scandal, but simply because he truly wished her to be his wife. Then, she might have been tempted. But she would not take advantage of his kindness and condemn them both to a loveless match.

"We will hold to our bargain. In a few weeks the season will be over, and we can put this behind us," she declared.

She knew as she said the words that they were a lie. True, once the season was over, she would return to Kent. In the autumn she would announce the end of the engagement and set Lord Endicott free with a clear conscience. But she knew she would never forget him, and the life of adventure that she had planned for herself no longer held quite the same allure as it once had.

Ten

After Lord Endicott took his leave, Diana and her mother spent the afternoon entertaining guests from last night's ball, who had come to pay their respects. George Wright's name was mentioned once or twice, but no one seemed to attach any special significance to him or to suspect his former association with Diana.

The days that followed proved strangely anticlimactic as Diana attended a few social engagements, two with Lord Endicott's escort and a handful without. There was no sign of George Wright.

Nor was there any sign that once again she was the target of malicious gossip. Instead, the only topic on everyone's lips was the news from the Continent. Rather than being swiftly defeated by the allies, Napoleon eluded the traps set for him, and his forces continued to grow as entire regiments defected to follow their former commander. New reports that he had amassed a huge army led by his famous Old Guard had struck fear into everyone's hearts. Few believed that Wellington and the allies could prevail against the French troops. Not when Wellington was handicapped by having to rely on raw troops, the best of his veterans having been dispatched earlier to America. Disaster seemed unavoidable, and those of the aristocracy who had flocked to the newly reopened Continent now streamed back into English ports, carrying their own predictions of gloom and doom.

All knew a great battle was imminent, one that might well decide the fate of the Continent. They waited in anxious silence for news, only to be cast into despair as reports came in that Napoleon had triumphed. Just as all seemed hopeless, their spirits were lifted by news of the Glorious Eighteenth of June. Wellington had not just been victorious; with the help of Blucher and his Prussians, they had crushed the French armies, dealing the final blow to Napoleon's ambitions.

It was the talk of London; indeed, no one could talk of anything else. Plans were made for enormous victory celebrations. Rumors swirled around the city that the allied monarchs were to come to London—even Tsar Alexander had condescended to join the festivities—and hostesses hastily calculated their chances of meeting and impressing the visiting monarchs.

In such an atmosphere it was little wonder that no one had the inclination to speculate upon the romances of a mere viscount and a country miss. Diana was grateful for the reprieve. But when her parents suggested that she might wish to stay in London through the summer, to take part in the extended season, Diana demurred. They would leave at the beginning of July as they had long planned. While it would be fascinating to meet such exotic foreign guests, she had no wish to remain in London for another month. Not when that meant she would have to prolong her public role as

Lord Endicott's fiancée, a role that grew more and more difficult to play with each day that passed.

It was not that she found the time spent with Lord Endicott to be distasteful. On the contrary, she found she liked it too well for her own comfort. The more time she spent with him, the harder it was to remember that they were only playacting. She had given him the chance to declare his feelings for her, but he had made it clear that his attentions came from his sense of duty. And so her own sense of honor demanded that she set him free at the end of the summer.

It was exactly one week after the engagement ball, on a sunny afternoon, that Diana journeyed to Hampstead Heath to attend a picnic hosted by Miss Charlotte Fox. It was a small, intimate gathering, with no more than two dozen ladies and gentlemen, along with Miss Fox's parents, who watched over the young ladies and gentlemen with fond approval. Lord Endicott had not been able to join her, having a previous commitment, but Diana had become friends with Miss Fox and her cousin, Anabelle Dawkins, and looked forward to spending a pleasant afternoon.

She was not pleased when she realized that George Wright was to be a member of the party. Too late she remembered his past friendship with Arthur Fox. Apparently young Mr. Fox had forgotten his earlier promise that he would no longer associate with Mr. Wright. So much for his sense of honor.

It was impossible for her to leave without causing a scene, so she resolved to simply put the best face on things that she could. Under the watchful eyes of the others, she exchanged polite greetings with George

Wright, who seemed impervious to her glare of disapproval. Arthur Fox soon drew George Wright away in conversation, and the party was large enough that there was no need for Diana to speak with him.

The word *picnic* implied a degree of informality, but this was far from the simple country affairs that Diana and her sisters had attended. Instead, tables had been set out on the grass and covered with white linen. The tables were set with silver, and they dined off fine china, enjoying the best delicacies that the Fox's chef had to offer. There were even ices provided for the ladies' delectation, carefully stored against the heat until just the right moment.

After lunch, small groups formed as the guests decided to stroll the park to take in the sights and perhaps to flirt decorously away from parental supervision. Diana and Miss Dawkins chose, instead, to sit underneath a shady tree, upon a wool blanket that had been provided for that very purpose. She watched as George Wright joined a group of gentlemen standing nearby, talking and sipping wine, relieved that he seemed to know enough to keep his distance.

"I vow I will never eat again," Miss Dawkins said, as she patted her slender waistline ruefully. "I should know better, but I can never resist lobster cakes. And did you taste the asparagus soup?"

"It was the ices that amazed me," Diana said. "To bring them all that way, in such heat, seems a fantastic luxury."

"They are Charlotte's favorite, and her parents can deny her nothing. Especially now when it seems that Lord Wiggams is finally ready to declare his intentions," Miss Dawkins said, nodding toward the couple as they strolled hand in hand by the ornamental pond.

"Charlotte must be relieved," Diana observed. Indeed, Lord Wiggams had been courting Charlotte Fox for nearly two years now. Charlotte had been patient but she had told her friends that if he did not come up to scratch by the end of the season; she would give him his marching orders and seek out a more decisive gentleman.

Her attention fixed on the courting couple, Diana did not hear George Wright's approach.

"Ladies," he said, with a bow. "I trust you are enjoying your afternoon?"

"Indeed, we are," Miss Dawkins replied.

Diana said nothing.

"Miss Somerville, would you be so kind as to accompany me for a turn about the lake?"

"No," Diana said, in a display of rudeness that would have been shocking under other circumstances.

"Yes, she will," Miss Dawkins said, rising to her feet. "I think that is a lovely idea."

"Anabelle," Diana said warningly.

"I see my aunt Laura is waving to me," Miss Dawkins said, not meeting Diana's gaze. "I must speak with her, and Mr. Wright can bear you company."

With that, Miss Dawkins began walking over to Mrs. Fox, who appeared to be quite contentedly conversing with her husband. Diana realized that she had been outmaneuvered and cursed Miss Dawkins under her breath. What was the girl thinking?

"If you do not wish to walk, I would be happy to join you here," Mr. Wright said.

Diana shook her head. She had no wish for the intimacy of sitting side by side upon a wool blanket with this man.

"If I tell you to go away, will you? As a gentleman should?"

"No," Mr. Wright said. She had not thought he would agree. "I came here today with the intention of claiming a few minutes of your time for private conversation. Surely you agree that there are things we must say to one another?"

"Anything you had to say should have been said months ago," Diana retorted. "For now, I think silence your best option."

"Come now, five minutes of your time," he said, extending his hand toward her. "I know I do not deserve such a favor, but I ask you to oblige me. As your future brother-in-law."

He stood there, his hand still extended toward her. She knew they made an odd tableau, and with a sigh of reluctance she rose to her feet, ignoring his outstretched hand. "Five minutes," she said.

She wondered what it was about him that he managed to get her to agree to things that she knew were wrong.

He picked up her parasol and handed it to her, waiting as she opened it and adjusted it against the sun. Then she began walking to the lake, and he fell in step beside her.

She had nothing to fear. They were in full view of the others, in a public place. All he could do was talk to her, and there was nothing he could say that would harm her.

Silence stretched between them, until she broke it "This was your idea. Speak," she commanded. "Or will return to the others."

"I have rehearsed this moment a hundred times, bu now words fail me," Mr. Wright said. "If we were i private I would fall to my knees. As it is, I can only stand here and tell you how much I regret my behavior. Wher I remember my actions on that night, I am ashamed o myself. I know I do not deserve your pardon, but I wan you to know that you have my heartfelt regrets."

She could not believe her ears. She glanced over a him and saw that his gaze was fixed firmly on the ground, his head low as if he were truly repentant.

"There can be no forgiveness for what you tried to do," Diana said, stunned by his effrontery. "And as for your apology, it is a little late, do you not think? Over two months too late."

"I understand your anger, and after today I wil never again inflict my presence upon you. I just wanted you to know how sorry I am."

"And this is supposed to change things?"

Their footsteps slowed, until they were standing at the edge of the pond. From here only their backs would be visible to the rest of the picnickers. There was no need to worry about what their expressions might reveal.

"I was drunk that night, though it is no excuse, I know. And I behaved impulsively, urged on by men of low character whom I had called friends. Indeed, so lost in depravity was I, that I brought you great harm. The next morning I could not bear to look at you, for in your eyes I saw reflected my own shame. Like a foolish boy I ran from London, letting my so-called friends convince me to join them on their journey to the Continent."

She listened, drawn into his narrative in spite of herself. She was surprised at his open admission of culpability and that he was not trying to make excuses for his conduct.

"And then? Why did you return?"

Mr. Wright turned sideways to face her.

"I could not stop thinking of you," he said, his voice trembling with emotion. "Every day you were in my thoughts, and the longer I stayed away, the more I realized that I was behaving as a coward. I came back to London to take responsibility for what I had done and to make amends in any way I could."

Her emotions were churning. One part of her insisted that his words were nothing but a self-serving lie, a pretty tale meant to regain her trust. But another part was not certain. He seemed so sincere in his misery, in his haunted expression and artless words.

"And you found me engaged to marry your brother," Diana said.

"In hindsight I suppose I should have expected it. Stephen has always been like that, always rushing in, even where he is not wanted. Just for once, I thought he would treat me like a man and let me take responsibility for my own actions. But, instead, he has robbed me of any chance of doing the honorable thing."

The bitterness in his voice was palpable.

"You would have offered to marry me?"

"Of course. It is why I returned. But, instead, I find I am not needed. Stephen has risen to the occasion.

Not that I blame you. The Viscount Endicott is a far better catch than I."

"I do not know what to say," Diana replied. His words had thrown her into confusion, and she no longer knew what to think. She remembered the other night and how she had thought George Wright a spoiled boy. And, indeed, there was truth to that observation. But was it because of a defect in his character? Or was his behavior caused by the fact that he had never been allowed to take on the responsibilities of a man?

"I wish you nothing but happiness," George said. "Both of you. I am certain my brother will make a fine husband. His sense of duty would not permit otherwise. And in time you will no doubt become accustomed to his rigid adherence to propriety."

There was a grain of truth to his words, and she knew it was fortunate that she did not, indeed, plan to be wed. Diana knew her streak of unconventionality would make her chafe at the dull and decorous life that Lord Endicott seemed to have lived before encountering her.

She wondered what George would say if she told him the engagement was a sham. Would he feel honor bound to offer himself in marriage? A part of her wished to hear him say the words, just so she could have the pleasure of rejecting him.

"I thank you for the courtesy of hearing me," Mr. Wright said. "Come now, let us rejoin the others. I promise that I will leave you in peace after today. But if you ever have need of my services, if there is ever anything I can do for you, know that I am at your disposal. You have only to ask."

The next night Diana and Lord Endicott joined the Dunnes in their box at the Italian Opera House. The featured singer this evening was an unknown, which mattered little save that it gave the society crowd even more excuse to ignore the events on stage and, instead, concentrate on observing those who were in attendance and gossiping about those who were not.

Diana waited until the Dunnes were deep in conversation before she turned to Lord Endicott and said, "I saw your brother yesterday. At a picnic in Hampstead Heath."

Lord Endicott clenched his jaw in disapproval. "The impudent rogue. I warned him against approaching you. I trust he knew better than to speak with you."

Diana waved her fan idly in one hand, ensuring that her expression was hidden from view of the occupants of the other boxes. "We did speak, and he was most civil. Surprisingly so, really."

"And what did he have to say?"

He implied you were an overbearing prig, Diana thought, but she could hardly say such. "He wished to beg my pardon."

"Too little, too late," Lord Endicott said with a growl.

"So I told him," Diana agreed. "But he felt he owed it to me to apologize, since it was not possible for him to make amends."

"He would have been better served to have left you in peace. As I instructed him," Lord Endicott said.

Diana shook her head in disagreement. "I think he was sincere in wishing to make peace between us," she said. "He knows what he did was wrong, and though we can never be friends, I think he hoped that we could behave civilly toward one another."

"You may be able to forgive him, but I cannot. Not today, not ever."

"I did not say that I forgave him," Diana said. Not yet. But she did not like Lord Endicott's ready condemnation of his brother. She was the injured party; surely it was up to her to decide if George Wright was sufficiently penitent for his actions. Lord Endicott's refusal to even consider such seemed overly harsh. This was his half brother after all, his flesh and blood.

She remembered how George had said that his brother was concerned with honor and propriety above all other sentiments, and now Lord Endicott had provided unwitting confirmation of his brother's accusation.

"George thinks we are to be married. Is it any wonder that he wishes a truce between our households?" Diana asked.

"I long ago ceased ascribing such noble motives to his behavior," Lord Endicott said. "You are letting your soft heart get the better of your judgment. Again."

She winced at the pointed reminder. True, she had been foolish in the past when she placed her trust in George Wright's honorable behavior. But it had been an innocent mistake, and it was petty of Lord Endicott to recollect such ancient history. She had paid for her folly, after all.

Diana furled her fan with a snap of her wrist. "I can see you are unable to discuss this matter rationally," she said.

"I am only thinking of you—"

"I prefer to think for myself," Diana retorted.

To this the viscount made no reply. Diana pointedly turned her back upon him, feigning interest in the occupants of the boxes on the far side of the theater. Recognizing the Fox family, Diana waved to them and was pleased when Charlotte Fox noticed her and waved her gloved hand in return.

Lord Endicott made a sound of protest, quickly choked off. No doubt he had noticed George Wright sitting in the box with the Foxes' party. No doubt he would think that she was favoring George. That had not been her intention, but she was not displeased with the results. Let Lord Endicott see her true nature. They might be engaged, but she was not some mindlessly obedient simpleton. She was an intelligent and rational creature, capable of deciding her own fate. It was time that both she and her spurious fiancé remembered that.

Eleven

Lord Endicott shook his head in bafflement. One moment he and Miss Somerville had been chatting pleasantly about the opera. And the next instant they had been quarreling, about his brother of all things.

George, who had deliberately flouted his brother's wishes and sought out Miss Somerville's company. And who apparently had used his glib tongue to convince Miss Somerville of the sincerity of his repentance. When he had tried to point out that she was allowing herself to be duped, by a man who had betrayed her once before, Miss Somerville's attitude had turned positively frosty.

Even now, as the singers massed on stage for the conclusion of the first half of the performance, Miss Somerville had turned away from him, conversing animatedly with Elizabeth Dunne. But he knew from the set of her back that Miss Somerville was angry with him—very angry—and he did not know how to remedy the situation.

As the lights rose for the intermission, many in the audience rose as well, hoping to stretch their legs or to visit acquaintances in the boxes.

"Ladies, shall we fetch champagne?" Tony Dunne asked.

"That would be lovely," Elizabeth Dunne replied. "If you do not mind, Diana and I will stay here. I have no wish to fight the crowds."

"Of course," Tony said, with a quick glance at his wife's face and waistline. Though no public announcement had been made, Stephen had learned only this week that the Dunnes were expecting their long-hoped-for second child. It was no wonder she had no wish to be jostled by the unruly crowds.

When he and Tony returned to the box, they found a small crowd had gathered, and they had to shoulder their way back in.

"Pardon me," Lord Endicott said, brushing aside one young fop. There were only a half dozen or so visitors, but they filled the tiny box to bursting.

He looked over the crowd and spotted Diana's dark head, nodding as if in agreement. And then he saw the sandy brown hair of her conversational partner, and he knew at once who it must be.

He swallowed hard, tasting bile. Was this really how it was to be? Could George have wormed his way back into Miss Somerville's graces so easily?

By dint of personality he managed to clear a path through the box and reached Diana.

"Your champagne," he said, handing her the glass flute.

"Thank you," Diana replied.

"George," he said coldly, giving his brother a frosty glare. "I did not expect to see you here."

"Miss Fox insisted on paying her respects, and as

her escort, I could hardly let her come alone," George replied. He smiled ruefully, as if inviting his brother to commiserate on the difficulties of catering to whims of the female sex.

"Miss Somerville told me of your encounter yesterday," Stephen said. He wondered if George could hear the warning in his words. Though there was little enough, in truth, that he could do to his brother. He had already warned him, banished him from Grosvenor Square, and withheld the advance upon his quarterly allowance that George had requested to pay off his many debts. There was nothing else he could do to control his brother, though a public flogging held more and more appeal.

"I am glad that she told you," George said. "I hope we now understand one another."

"I think we understand one another perfectly," Stephen said. He did not know what game George was playing at, only that whatever scheme he had up his sleeve, it was sure to bode no good for anyone.

Diana stood equidistant between them, her gaze unreadable. He found himself wishing that she would come stand beside him, in a show of public support.

He heard the ringing of a bell and the attendants moving through the halls calling out that the performance was about to recommence.

"I have taken enough of your time," George said to Diana. He picked up her hand, and Stephen watched in disbelief as she actually let him brush it with his lips. Then he relinquished it with every sign of reluctance. What would have been a polite courtesy in another gentleman seemed an obscene act, given George's past treatment of Diana.

Then he turned to Stephen. "Brother," he said.

"George," Stephen replied stiffly. He would not call this man brother.

"Give my regards to my mother," George said. "Since I seldom have the opportunity to see her these days."

"I will speak of you to Caroline," Stephen promised, though he intended to do far more than simply pass along George's regards. He would speak bluntly with Caroline about her son and see if she could convince him of the folly of his present course. If George continued to pester Miss Somerville, Stephen would have no choice but to take drastic action.

Diana was surprised to receive an invitation to take tea with Lady Endicott, for despite having hosted a ball in celebration of the engagement, the dowager viscountess had shown little interest in her future daughter-in-law. Nor had Stephen shown any interest in having her become better acquainted with his stepmother; indeed, he deliberately seemed to be keeping them apart. Strange, too, that his stepmother was not privy to the facts of their engagement, while his closest friends, the Dunnes, had been told the truth.

Even more intriguing was the postscript requesting that Diana come alone, without her mother. It was either a mark of rudeness or a sign that Lady Endicott wished to impart confidences that were best aired in private. And so it was with great curiosity that Diana ventured to the viscount's residence in Grosvenor Square on the appointed day.

A liveried footman wearing an old-fashioned powdered wig greeted her at the door.

"The viscountess is expecting you," he said. "If you would follow me, I will show you to the Chinese drawing room."

He led the way down the hall, pausing outside the door to knock once, and then he opened it.

"Miss Somerville," he announced, as if there was any doubt.

As Diana entered the room, her eyes were struck at once by the crimson-and-gold-colored walls and the sofas and settees which were upholstered to match. Two enormous blue-and-white vases flanked either side of the fireplace, while the mantel above displayed carved figurines of ivory. More vases and jade statues were found on the small tables that cluttered the room. It was as if she had stepped into a room in the palace of a Chinese emperor, and she marveled at the time and skill it must have taken to amass such a collection.

"Miss Somerville, it is so good of you to come," Lady Endicott said, rising from her seat on the sofa. "Please, take a seat."

"Lady Endicott, thank you for inviting me," Diana said.

She stepped carefully around a table displaying an ivory and jade chess set and gazed longingly at a curio cabinet before she took a seat opposite her hostess.

"Pardon my staring, but you have so many beautiful things in this room," Diana explained.

"You are most kind," Lady Endicott said, with a

smile. "This room is a favorite of mine. Most of the objets d'art in here were gifts from my late husband, and for that reason I treasure them."

"He had exquisite taste," Diana replied.

"In all things," Lady Endicott agreed.

She poured a cup of tea into a porcelain cup that was so delicately fashioned that it was nearly translucent. Diana accepted it carefully, thinking that such beauty belonged on display rather than being used for an everyday occasion.

Or perhaps this was not an ordinary occasion, she reminded herself, as the viscountess poured her own tea. The two of them busied themselves adding cream and sugar and then exchanged the expected pleasantries. Diana offered the good wishes of her mother and father, neither of whom were aware of her presence here today. For her part, Lady Endicott expressed herself eager to better their acquaintance.

As they chatted pleasantly about trifles, Diana took the opportunity to study her hostess. Sunlight was not as kind to Lady Endicott as the candlelit glow of a ballroom, but she was still quite beautiful for a woman who must be nearing forty years of age. Her blond hair showed not the slightest trace of gray, and her French silk gown was in the height of fashion.

It was not till they had finished their tea that Lady Endicott turned the conversation toward more serious matters.

"I asked you here today so that we could get to know one another, since we are to be so closely related," Lady Endicott said, putting down her tea cup upon the tray. "But I will admit to another motive as well."

"Yes?" Diana prompted.

"I want to ask your help in healing the rifts between my sons," Lady Endicott said.

This was something Diana had not expected. She had wondered at the reason for this meeting and supposed it might be natural curiosity. Lady Endicott might simply wish to quiz her in private, wondering how it was that Diana and Stephen had become acquainted. Or, if somehow word of the scandal had reached her ears, Lady Endicott might have intended to question Diana about it. She had even imagined that Lady Endicott might wish to apologize for any pain that George had inflicted. But never had she imagined that the viscountess would ask Diana to play the role of peacemaker.

"I don't understand," Diana said, as the silence stretched on between them.

"Surely you must have noticed at the ball there was some awkwardness between them," Lady Endicott said.

"I am afraid that I did not notice," Diana lied. "In truth, I was overwhelmed by the excitement of the evening."

Lady Endicott gave her a shrewd look and then sighed. "You must understand that I was but a girl when I married Lord Endicott. And though there were fifteen years between us, it was, indeed, a love match, and we cared for each other greatly. But from the very first, young Stephen resented me."

"I suppose he missed his own mother," Diana said.

"Of course, and I tried my best to make it up to him. But the harder I tried, the more stubbornly he pushed me away. It was worse when George was born. Rather than being pleased at having a new brother, he resented every minute that his father or I spent with the baby."

It was difficult to imagine. How could anyone not like having a new brother? Diana had been thrilled each time her mother had presented the family with a new sister, her only disappointment that none of them was the brother that they hoped for.

"No doubt it was hard for him to share your attention. After all, he was the only child for eight years," Diana said, feeling she had to defend him.

"We thought it was just a childish whim and that he would soon outgrow it," Lady Endicott said. "Andrew and I tried hard to treat both boys equally, but Stephen was always jealous. Whatever George had, Stephen had to have as well. When George was given a pony, Stephen demanded a new hunter. If George had a set of toy soldiers, Stephen needed the same, no matter that he was too old for such childishness. As the boys grew older, it became worse. George worshipped his older brother and could never understand why Stephen rebuffed his every offer of friendship."

Lady Endicott painted a grim picture, indeed, but one that was all too plausible. A grieving widower, his young wife, and the only child who found himself no longer the center of his father's attention. Many a boy might have acted as she described. But it was hard to reconcile these images with the man that she had come to know. The Stephen she knew was invariably kind and thoughtful. He had displayed infinite patience when dealing with Diana's younger sisters. She found it hard to believe that he could have behaved as badly as Lady Endicott seemed to imply.

"But surely they are both gentlemen now and of an age to mend any childish quarrels," Diana protested.

"So one would hope. And in time they might have mended things, if my husband had lived. As it was, he died most unexpectedly, leaving Stephen the burden of the title when he was barely one and twenty. His new stature quite went to his head, and Stephen became even more dictatorial and controlling. It was no wonder that George rebelled. With neither father nor brother to guide him, I fear greatly that my son may fall into unsavory company."

Lady Endicott took a handkerchief out of her sleeve and dabbed at her pale blue eyes. "A mother worries so," she explained.

And she was right to worry, though Diana had no intention of being the one to tell Lady Endicott that her precious son was well on his way to becoming an incorrigible rake having tried to ruin a young gentlewoman to satisfy a drunken wager. Diana could not make such an accusation without revealing that she herself had been the intended victim.

It was no wonder that Lady Endicott had such a biased view of Stephen's behavior. Diana wondered how many other scandals George had caused that his mother had remained oblivious to. Lady Endicott saw only Stephen's efforts to rein in his brother, without understanding the reasons why Stephen acted as he did. It was a dilemma, to be certain, but it was not her place to solve it.

"And you wish my help?" Diana asked.

"Yes," Lady Endicott replied. "I will admit that the news of your engagement came as a surprise, for Stephen had never even mentioned you to me. But then I realized that your marriage would be a blessing for us all. Once he has a family of his own, Stephen will no longer have any reason to be jealous of George. You can help him see the light and to appreciate George's many fine qualities."

Diana doubted that very much. Merely mentioning George's name was enough to make Stephen's jaw clench with anger. And she had her own quarrel with George that made her disinclined to advance his cause.

"Stephen, that is, Lord Endicott, is a good man. An honorable man," Diana said. "I know that he can be trusted to do what is right by his family."

And there was little enough she could do. If she were to marry Stephen, then that would be a different story. Then, given time, she might be able to influence the behavior of both brothers. But as a temporary fiancée, her powers of persuasion were, indeed, limited.

"Of course. And I hope I have not distressed you with my candor."

"Not at all. You have given me much to think about," Diana said.

Now she just had to decide what, if anything, she would tell Stephen of this meeting. Or perhaps she would be better served to keep her own counsel. Time and observation would prove or disprove Lady Endicott's assertions, and then Diana would make up her own mind on what course of action she should take.

* * *

On Monday evenings the Explorers' club served sir-
loins of beef, and in the height of the season it was no
surprise to find the dining room filled to capacity.
When he arrived, Lord Endicott was shown to a table
where his friends were already seated. They greeted
him amiably, remarking on how seldom he had been
seen at the club this season. He explained that he had
been uncommonly busy, which drew nods of understanding and reassurances that once he was wed, there
would be no need to dance constant attendance upon
his wife.

Fortunately the servants chose that moment to bring
the main course, saving him from the necessity of
making a reply. As they devoured the excellent beef, a
reverent hush fell over the table, testimony to the
chef's great skill. It was not until the main courses
were cleared away that the conversation once again
became general. Stephen toyed with his fork, barely
touching the sweet set before him.

He felt curiously disconnected from this place, as if
he were an observer in his own body. It was strange.
These Monday dinners had been part of the ritual of
his existence for years now, and yet on this night he
wondered why he had bothered to come. Even the
things that had once brought him pleasure now seemed
dull and lifeless. Twice he looked up and found Tony
Dunne's eyes resting on him, his face showing concern. But they were seated at opposite ends of the table, so he was safe from interrogation.

After what seemed an eternity, the sweet course was
cleared away, and the diners arose. Mr. Smythe and Mr.
Campbell took their leave, no doubt bound for some

gaming hell or another. The rest expressed their intention of retiring to the library for brandy and cigars.

Tony Dunne caught his eye. "Shall we play a hand
or two of piquet?" he asked.

Stephen shrugged. "Why not?"

He had no wish to play at cards, but neither did he
wish to return to the house in Grosvenor Square and to
his solitary thoughts.

He followed Tony up the stairs and into the blue
parlor, which was quiet at this time of the evening.
Save for Lord Grimthorpe, who dozed quietly by the
fireplace, the room was empty.

A footman brought a fresh pack of cards and placed
a brandy decanter and two goblets on the table beside
them.

He wondered if Tony would press him, but his friend
seemed content to let him be, talking only as the game
dictated. Stephen tried to lose himself in the play; but
his mind wandered, and it was no surprise when Tony
Dunne took the final trick and won the round.

"Again?" Tony asked, gathering up the cards.

"Yes," Stephen said, reaching for his goblet. He
raised it to his lips, but only tasted the brandy before
setting it down. He knew instinctively that the answers
he sought were not to be found in a brandy glass.

They played for a few moments, and then suddenly
he could take no more of this. He ided his cards
together and set them carefully down on the table. "I
am losing her," he confessed.

Tony Dunne set down his own cards. "What do you
mean?"

Stephen kept his gaze fixed upon the brightly colored playing cards. It was easier to talk this way. "Miss Somerville. I am losing her, and I don't know what to do."

He waited for Tony Dunne to remind him of what they both knew. That Miss Somerville had never been his to lose in the first place. That they had entered into their arrangement both knowing it was a temporary affair, a deception meant to fool society. But, instead, he had been the one fooled. He had tried to convince society that they were in love, and, instead, he had convinced himself.

"You do not wish her to return to Kent?" Tony Dunne asked.

Stephen shook his head. "Actually, I would be happy to see her back in her home. Circumstances being what they are, I urged her father not to delay their departure, but, instead, to leave as planned."

"The circumstances being your brother's arrival."

"Yes," Stephen confirmed. He did not trust George and was convinced that his brother had it in mind to work some great mischief. But Miss Somerville had no intention of heeding his cautions. "When Diana found that I had spoken to her father, she was furious. She told me that I had no right to do so and that I was a high-handed brute for trying to dictate her life. Said she had no intention of leaving London and missing the excitement of the visiting foreign royals."

"But you are her fiancé."

"For now," Stephen said. "She offered to release me from the engagement at once if her behavior displeased me."

"Naturally you refused."

"Of course." Stephen ran one hand through his hair. "I do not know what to do. A fortnight ago I was certain we were approaching an understanding. I planned to ask her to marry me in truth. And then George returned, and everything changed."

Tony Dunne gazed at him keenly and then reached over to the decanter and refilled his glass. He contemplated the brandy in silence before lifting his eyes to his friend. When he spoke, his gaze was full of compassion. "Have you considered that this may be for the best? If Miss Somerville is so easily swayed, then she is not the woman for you."

"No," Stephen replied without thinking. The fault lay not with Miss Somerville, but with himself. He should have spoken of his feelings, convinced her of the sincerity of his regard. Instead, he had courted her slowly, not wishing to frighten her off. He had hoped that in time she would see how well suited they were for each other and agree to become his wife.

"She does not want me. I am too dull, too conservative for her tastes. She wants excitement. She wants George, and she is ready to forgive his misdeeds."

The thought left a bitter taste in his mouth. How could she be so naive? George had callously tried to ruin Diana. And yet, such was his charm that with a few glib speeches and show of contrition, he was well on the way to regaining Miss Somerville's trust. Not that Diana was foolish, but rather her own good nature blinded her to the wickedness of others. Such innocence made her easy prey here in London. He shuddered to think what would happen if she was ever able to fulfill her dream of traveling the world.

"So what do you plan to do? Will you just stand aside, and let George take her?"

He had spent two sleepless nights pondering this very question. He did not know what to do. Diana would not listen to reason, and if he pressed much harder, he was afraid that she would carry through on her threat and notify the papers that the engagement was at an end. And then he would have no opportunity to see her at all.

And as for his brother, there was another dilemma.

"I tried to buy him off," Stephen said. "Offered him a thousand pounds to leave England and return to the Continent. But he refused. Said he wouldn't leave for ten thousand pounds."

He had been certain that his brother would accept the bribe. Money had always worked with George before, and a thousand pounds was more than George's annual allowance. But it seemed this time his brother had something different in mind.

"If he is not willing to leave, then perhaps you have misjudged him. Perhaps he does, indeed, love this Miss Somerville, in his own way."

"No," Stephen said. "That I will not believe."

"You could always have him kidnapped. Find some captain heading to India or the Orient and pay him to take on an unwilling passenger," Tony suggested.

"Do not tempt me." He had already thought of this himself. He supposed it was a measure of his desperation that he was willing to consider such dishonorable actions.

"Then, what shall you do?"

"What I can. Watch. Wait. Be her friend, if she will

let me," he said. He could not let her go, and he refused to let George win. Somehow, he would find a
way to convince her that he was the only man for her.

Nearly a week had passed since she had taken tea
with the dowager Lady Endicott, and Diana still did
not know what to make of the viscountess's remarks.
The picture she had painted of Stephen as a brooding
and jealous older brother was a grim one, indeed. A
part of Diana wanted to dismiss it out of hand, and yet
another part could not help wondering if there was at
least a grain of truth in what Lady Endicott had said.
It was against Diana's nature to be suspicious of anyone, and yet clearly here someone must be lying or, at
the very least, bending the truth to suit their own purpose.

And then there was Stephen, who rather than playing the sinister role assigned to him was acting as a
perfect gentleman, seeming to belie his stepmother's
words. He had apologized to Diana for their quarrel at
the opera, saying that he had been wrong to doubt her
judgment. To make up for his sins, he had offered to
teach her to drive a whiskey-gig, and his kindness
made her feel all the more wretched for harboring sus-
picions about his motives.

If only there was someone she could trust, an impar-
tial bystander who would help her tell truth from false-
hood. But there was no one she could turn to. Stephen
was hardly a neutral party, and yet she longed to confide in him. Still, she knew instinctively that he would
be displeased to learn that she had discussed him with

his stepmother, and she had no wish to quarrel with
him. She shivered as she imagined how angry he
would be if she tried to discover whether there was any
truth in his stepmother's accusations.

"Are you cold? We can do this another day," Lord
Endicott said.

"No," Diana replied, summoning up a bright smile.
"The fog will soon burn off, and I would not miss this
for anything."

It was just past eight o'clock, and the fashionable
streets in London were empty, many of their residents
still in their beds after staying out till nearly dawn.
Green Park would be all but empty at this hour, which
was why Lord Endicott had chosen it for her driving
lesson. He was far too cautious to let her try her skills
during the afternoon, when the park would be crowded
with the fashionable set. But perhaps, after she had had
a lesson or two, she could convince him to let her drive
during the afternoon promenade. She imagined the
look of astonishment and envy upon the faces of the
other young women of the *ton,* as they saw Diana ex-
pertly tooling the carriage along the crowded path-
ways.

The gates of Green Park loomed up through the fog,
and the carriage passed between them. A few yards
inside the gate, Lord Endicott drew the gig to a stop,
and the groom hopped off the rear seat and went to
hold the horse's head.

Lord Endicott set the whip into a small holder and
then pulled up a wooden lever on the left-hand side of
the coach. "The hand brake," he explained. "Though
it will not hold a horse if he chooses to bolt, which is

why I bring Jim along, to hold the horse when I stop the carriage."

Diana nodded. This much she already knew.

"You have driven a pony cart, yes?" Lord Endicott asked.

"Yes," Diana replied. Several years before, her father had given in to her pleading and taught her to drive the pony cart. She had often driven her sisters into the village or to pay calls upon a neighboring estate. But the cart was a slow, four-wheeled contraption, and the pony that pulled it was a placid beast, who had never galloped in his life. A far cry from the two-wheeled gig and the fine thoroughbred that Lord Endicott drove. At this moment she was grateful that Lord Endicott had chosen the whiskey-gig, rather than the highly fashionable and equally unstable curricle.

"The principle is the same," Lord Endicott said. "But you will find that Ajax here requires more sensitive handling than a pony. And the whiskey-gig is lighter than a cart, which means he can set a fast pace, when needed."

"How fast can he go?"

"We will not find out today," Lord Endicott said. "Let us try simply to make a circuit of the park without mishap, shall we?"

"Very well."

Lord Endicott moved his grip so he held one rein in each hand, and then he drew them toward her. "Here, put your hands on the reins, just above mine," he said.

Diana leaned forward slightly and grasped the reins. She was conscious suddenly of his nearness, his side pressing against hers, and his large, capable hands seemingly dwarfing hers. It was a dizzying sensation, and for a moment she could not concentrate.

She took a deep breath. "I have them," she said.

Lord Endicott removed his own hands from the reins.

"Good. Let's try this at a walk. Jim," he called, and the groom let go of the horse's head and climbed on the back.

"Ready?"

"Yes," Diana said, trying to ignore the butterflies that had taken up residence inside her stomach.

Lord Endicott released the hand brake and then placed his own hands over hers. She could feel the heat of them even through the kid leather gloves she wore. "Shake the reins once, and Ajax will know to walk on."

Diana did so, and the horse obediently set off at a rather tame walk. Lord Endicott's hands rested lightly over hers, steadying her as she became accustomed to the sensation. The reins were far lighter than she was accustomed to, and Ajax was exceptionally well trained, for he moved at the slightest touch. When the path split into two, it took only a subtle pressure on the right rein, and he turned himself obediently down the right-hand path.

Diana beamed over at Lord Endicott. "See? I knew I could do this," she announced.

"Keep your eyes on the path," he said. But he smiled back at her and released his hands so that she was driving on her own.

Diana felt a thrill of exhilaration, realizing that this

magnificent conveyance was, indeed, under her control. It was better than she had ever imagined, and she pitied the young ladies who lived their whole lives without ever once having experienced this for themselves. They made three circuits of the park, two at a walk, and the final one at a smooth trot. Lord Endicott was endlessly patient, even when she misjudged a turn, causing the carriage to leave the pathway for a moment, leaving wheel tracks upon the dew-soaked grass. He waited until she had guided Ajax back onto the path before reminding her that when moving swiftly she needed to keep looking ahead, to give her plenty of time to maneuver.

When they finished the third circuit, the fog had, indeed, burned off, and there were now a handful of people strolling along, enjoying their morning constitutional, as well as a few other carriages. But there was no one she recognized who could bear witness to her daring.

"Again? Please?" Diana asked.

"Not today," Lord Endicott said. "We should stop now, before your arms get tired and you make a mistake."

Reluctantly Diana handed him back the reins, and as she flexed her hands, she discovered that they were, indeed, tired. And her shoulders were slightly sore, but these minor aches meant nothing when compared with the excitement of her experience.

"That was wonderful," she said.

"I am glad that you enjoyed it," Lord Endicott replied. "It is my pleasure to please you."

"And you have done so very well," Diana replied.

Her happiness and the bright sunshine combined to dispel her earlier doubts, and she felt in perfect charity with him as he drove her back to Chesterfield Hill.

Twelve

"Would you care to see a copy of *Guy Mannering*? It is by the same author who penned *Waverly* and is considered every bit its equal." The young clerk beamed at her hopefully, holding up a thick volume bound in red leather.

Diana shook her head. "I have no taste for novels."

The clerk's eyes widened at this revelation. No doubt he was accustomed to the more usual young ladies who patronized Hatchard's, devouring every novel and silly Minerva Press tale they could get their hands on.

"I was hoping to find a copy of Cook's account of his explorations of the South Seas," she said.

"Been some time since there's been any call for such, miss," the clerk said. "Seeing as how the captain has been dead nigh unto forty years now."

"Thirty-six years, actually," Diana corrected him. "And would you check for me? Please."

With a heavy sigh indicating that he was doing so only out of his innate generosity, the young clerk disappeared into the back storage room, where the public was not allowed. Diana strolled over to a mahogany case displaying the latest offerings from the London publishers. Her gaze wandered over the brightly bound novels and hastily printed pamphlets describing the victory of Waterloo, hoping for more serious fare.

Her eye was caught by a slim volume which was entitled "A True Tale of the Astounding Journeys of Messrs. Meriwether Lewis and William Clark, as they mapped the Uncharted Wildernesses of the American Territories." As she reached for the book, her arm was jostled by a gentleman reaching for one of the pamphlets.

"I beg your pardon," she said. She turned, and her heart gave a jump as she recognized the gentleman who now stood beside her.

"No, it is I who beg your pardon. Again," George Wright replied. "Miss Somerville, it is a pleasure to see you."

"Mr. Wright," she said coolly.

George Wright reached forward and plucked the volume from the shelf and handed it to her with a bow. "Is this what you were reaching for?"

"Yes, thank you," she said.

"I should have guessed," he replied. "I know your love for learning of foreign lands."

Diana was in a quandary. It seemed strange to be conversing with George Wright as if they were old friends, but then again what was she to do? This was a public place, and she could hardly order him to leave. Nor did she wish to leave, not until she had concluded her business here.

She was saved by the return of the young clerk, who carried in his arm a half dozen dust-covered volumes.

"I have the set, all six volumes, including the quarto with maps and drawings," the clerk announced.

"Excellent," Diana said, with a beaming smile. This was one of the true advantages of London. The small circulating library near her home had only a limited collection of books, and she had read everything of interest several times over. But here in London, she was free to indulge herself to her heart's delight, spending her pin money on tales of exotic lands.

The clerk set his finds on the counter and then reached into his pocket and pulled out a handkerchief which he used to mop his brow. "Would you like these on account?" he asked.

"Yes, and this as well," Diana said, handing him the book she had found. "Miss Somerville, of number fourteen, Chesterfield Hill. If you would be so good as to have these sent round."

"They will be there before nightfall," the clerk promised.

George Wright stood patiently behind her as the clerk wrapped up the parcel, and Diana signed the ticket.

"May I offer you an escort anywhere?" he asked.

"No, thank you. This was my last errand, and I am about to return home," Diana said.

George winced. "And I would not be welcome there."

"Well, no, er, that is—" Diana floundered. In truth, she knew George would not be welcome, and should her father be home, no doubt there would be a very awkward and unpleasant scene. It was no more than George deserved, and yet somehow, when confronted with his presence, it was hard to remember the anger toward him that had once burned so hotly inside her.

"Do not fret yourself," he said. "I understand."

Perversely the more he reassured her, the worse she felt. He opened the door for her, and she stepped out onto the street. Her maid, Jenna, who had been sitting on a bench outside the door, rose and came over to join her mistress.

"I hope I did not cause any trouble between you and my brother the other night," George said. "He seemed distressed to find me in your box at the theater."

Distressed was putting it delicately. Stephen had been positively enraged. And then, when she had attempted to explain, he had turned high-handed and dictatorial, refusing to listen to her. Then, not content to give orders to her, he had gone behind her back, urging her parents to leave London for the country. It was humiliating to realize that he did not trust her virtue or her common sense.

Diana had put Lord Endicott squarely in his place. She had convinced her parents to remain in London through July and informed the arrogant viscount that she was prepared to end the engagement at once, should he find himself inconvenienced.

"Your brother has firm opinions," Diana said.

"And he does not wish me to see you," George said. "Though that seems folly since you are to be my sister-in-law. Still, it is all of a piece with him. Over these years, I have learned to expect little in the way of consideration from him."

His voice was sad, as if resigned to his brother's failings, and Diana was reminded of the confidences that Lady Endicott had shared over tea only a few days before. Could there be some truth to the dowager viscountess's words? Had there always been bad blood between the brothers? And if so, what did that say to Stephen's motives in seeking her out? Was it simply a matter of honor, or was there some other reason why he had pursued her?

"Perhaps, if you can find it in your heart to forgive me, some day he can forgive me as well. I want nothing more than to be able to call him a true brother," George declared.

Diana winced inwardly. Were she truly to marry his brother, then, indeed, she might be forced into the role of peacemaker. As it was, given how strained her own relations were with Lord Endicott, nothing she said was likely to advance his brother's cause.

"If you behave yourself with propriety and refrain from scandal, I am certain your brother will come to see you in a new light," she said. She herself was still uncertain as to George's character. Was his repentance genuine, his crime against her a youthful folly he now regretted deeply? Or was he still a rake who cared for nothing but himself, as Lord Endicott averred?

George smiled. "I can but try. And in that light, may I take you for ices at Gunther's? It is too fine a day to rush indoors."

Diana hesitated. The day was, indeed, sunny and warm, and ices had become a secret passion of hers.

"I assure you I will behave myself as a gentleman," he said, with a boyish grin. "Please?"

"Yes, thank you, I would like that very much," Diana said. After all, she had her maid with her, and there was nothing at all improper about a gentleman escorting a lady to Gunther's for ices. Lord Endicott had taken her twice, and more often she had gone with a group of young ladies and gentlemen who now formed her acquaintance.

They strolled together over to Oxford Street, followed by the dutiful Jenna. Upon reaching Gunther's tea shop, George found them a place at an outdoor table and then went inside to procure refreshments, returning with strawberry sorbets for himself and Diana and a glass of lemonade for Jenna, who accepted the largesse gratefully and then seated herself on a nearby bench, along with a half dozen other maids and a pair of footmen.

As she took a spoonful of sorbet, Diana's first impression was of blissful coolness. Only as it melted in her mouth could she then taste the sweetness of the strawberry flavoring. It was a perfect treat for a summer's afternoon, and as she smiled in bliss, George beamed back at her in perfect accord.

In between bites of the sorbet, they spoke of mutual acquaintances and the latest on-dits. Unlike his brother's habitual reserve, George was an accomplished conversationalist, at ease discussing any topic. They bantered easily, discovering a great similarity in their opinions. Both of them loathed the opera, but loved the theater. They agreed Lady Shenton's new town house was the height of vulgarity and that the fireworks celebrating the victory at Waterloo had been a wonder beyond imagining.

She quizzed George on his recent sojourn in France. Not for the first time she envied the freedom that came with his gender. She and George were nearly the same age, and yet propriety dictated that as a woman she remain sheltered by her family, while George was free to roam the world over should he choose to do so.

"It is a pity your journey was cut so short," Diana said.

George shook his head. "I should not have left at all," he said solemnly.

Diana felt her cheeks color as the implications of his words sank in. She had not meant her words to sound like an accusation.

"I did not mean—" she began, and then fell short.

George reached across the table and took her gloved hand in his own. "I know you did not mean to accuse me. I accuse myself," he said. "I thought of you constantly, you know. I remembered how much you longed to travel. In Calais, and Lille, and in Brussels, I kept thinking how much you would have enjoyed seeing these cities and how I longed to be the one to show them to you. And the more I thought of you, the more the guilt grew in me, and I knew I should never have left you."

Rather than reassuring her, his constant repentance made Diana feel as if she were somehow the guilty party.

"I thought we agreed to put the past behind us," she said.

"Of course."

He relinquished her hand as a waiter arrived to clear away the dishes. Diana took advantage of the interruption to change the conversation to a more neutral topic.

"Are you decided to stay in England? Or will you be

rejoining your friends and resuming your travels?" she
asked.

"I thought to stay in England, at least until your
wedding this fall. After that, I do not know. And yourself? Are you to remain in London this summer? Or
will you be returning to Kent to make your preparations?"

She squirmed inside, wondering how George would
react when the engagement was called off. Would he
understand her decision? Or would he try to court her
again? After all, he had returned to England with the
intent of offering for her.

But she could hardly marry him, no matter what
feelings she had once harbored for him. George might
be a kindred spirit, but she did not love him. And she
had already caused enough scandal. Breaking with
Lord Endicott only to marry his half brother would
undo everything they had worked so hard to achieve,
and would be poor repayment of Lord Endicott's generosity.

"We will remain in London, through the end of this
month at least. After that, I am not certain what my
parents intend," Diana temporized. She could hardly
admit that there was no need to rush home, since there
was not actually going to be a wedding.

"Good," George said. "Did you know that the Tsar
Alexander and members of his court are soon to arrive? He and his sister, the grand duchess, are to be
Prinny's guests. Not to mention General Blucher and
his Prussians."

Indeed, London society could talk of nothing else,
eagerly awaiting the arrival of the foreign royals. Such

an event had not occurred in generations, and society hostesses everywhere were frantically scheming to be the first to host the noble visitors.

"I hope to meet with some of our visitors, to hear of their homelands and their impressions of England. After all, to them this will be a foreign country," Diana said.

"If you allow, I will be happy to arrange introductions," George said. "I met many members of the court while in Brussels, including Count Peter Kossilof, who has the honor of serving as an attendant to the tsar. I am certain he would be willing to introduce you to other members of the court, who would be happy to speak with you."

"Thank you," Diana said. This was generous, indeed, for there would be many clamoring for introductions to their illustrious visitors. And it would be useful for her to have acquaintances in foreign cities, once she embarked upon her career as an explorer.

"It is nothing," George said. "Remember, I swore to be at your service."

Lord Hawksley's carriage bounced as it hit a patch of uneven pavement, and Stephen braced one arm against the side of the seat to steady himself. Honestly, the streets of London grew worse every year, despite the vast sums spent for their improvement. Across from him, Lord Hawksley did not even pause in his speech, seeming oblivious to the jolting and swaying of his ancient carriage as it bore them toward the

Houses of Parliament and the latest committee meeting of the Tory party leaders.

"I have it upon good authority that the Whigs are planning to bestow even more honors upon Wellington, after his latest triumph," Lord Hawksley continued. "We must be certain that the Tories do not lag behind in recognizing our great hero. We must make it clear to all that he is one of our own."

"But what more honors can they award? He is already a duke and has received every medal the Regent and Parliament can devise. Short of renaming the city Wellingtonville, I do not know what else we can do."

Lord Hawksley lifted his bushy gray eyebrows and peered disapprovingly at his companion. "This is a serious topic, not one for jest," he said. "With the threat of Napoleon now gone, we must move swiftly to consolidate our political power, both at home and upon the Continent. Alliances made now will secure power for the next generation."

"I bow to your experience in these matters, Lord Hawksley," he said.

In truth, he had little interest in politics, outside of those that affected his own county. But Stephen's father had been a prominent Tory, and when he had inherited his title, Stephen had also inherited his father's politics and his political allies. Such as Lord Hawksley, a dyed-in-the-wool conservative, whose political views had not changed one iota in the last half century.

"There is talk of making Wellington an ambassador," Lord Hawksley said. "To keep him in France, until the allies can sort out the mess that Bonaparte made of the Continent. Make him our lead negotiator."

"His presence would be a potent reminder of how much the Continent owes to British military power," Stephen agreed.

"Without us they would have been speaking French from Sicily to St. Petersburg," Lord Hawksley said disdainfully. "We secured the peace and ensured the stability of the monarchies. Now it is time to reap our just rewards."

There was sense in what he said. The allies had worked together to defeat Napoleon, but now with their common enemy gone, the former allies would each be jockeying for power and position in the New European order. No doubt the coming negotiations would require every bit as much cunning and strategy as the hard-fought military campaign.

Stephen listened with half an ear as Lord Hawksley continued to expound upon his plans for the coming debate. In truth, there was little required of him, save to nod at the appropriate intervals. He gazed out the carriage window as they drove down Oxford Street. A strolling couple caught his eye. Though he could see only their backs, there was something familiar about the woman's figure. As the carriage drew abreast, he lost sight of the couple in a crowd. He turned and looked backward, and smiled as he recognized Miss Somerville. He would know her anywhere.

Then his gaze turned toward her companion, and his jaw clenched as he recognized his brother. Anger welled up within him. What on earth was George doing with Diana? How dare he even speak to her, let alone accost her on a public street? Had he no sense of decency?

And what of Diana? For she did not appear distressed, nor did it appear that she was making any attempt to avoid George's company. His eyes narrowed as he saw that Diana's gloved hand rested lightly on George's arm as he walked beside her.

Stephen leaned forward, ready to command that the carriage be stopped, intent upon confronting the two of them. Then, just as swiftly as the impulse came, it passed. If he saw George now, he would not be able to control himself, and the resulting scene would hardly improve his chances with Miss Somerville. This was no accidental encounter; on the contrary, Diana showed every sign of being with George by choice. However loathsome Stephen found that idea, he could not dictate Diana's every waking hour.

He did not know how Diana would react if he were to confront her in such a public setting. No doubt she would be humiliated and justly angry with him. He already knew that she had a stubborn streak. And were he to demand that she cease seeing George, she might well carry out her threat to end their engagement. Then he would have no excuse to see her and be forced to watch helplessly from the sidelines as George betrayed her for a second time.

He did not understand, Stephen thought, sinking back against the worn seats as the pair faded from sight. He had treated Miss Somerville with respect, courting her in hopes of winning her affection. And yet it was his rakehell brother, George, to whom she was drawn, a man who had treated her dishonorably once and seemed likely to do so again. Surely there had to

e something Stephen could do to convince her of the
incerity of his admiration.

He sighed.

"Is there something wrong?" Lord Hawksley asked,
reaking off in mid-diatribe.

"Yes," Stephen said. "Or rather, no. Nothing that
eed concern you. A dilemma of my own making, as it
vere."

Lord Hawksley's gaze sharpened. "Affairs of the
eart are never easy. They make politics look simple."

The keen insight surprised him. Was he really that
asy to read? Or was Lord Hawksley more perceptive
han he had given him credit for? Stephen was uncom-
ortable with the idea that his thoughts could be read
o easily.

"Each man must tend to his own affairs," said
Stephen, firmly closing the subject. "Now, tell me,
vhat do you think of young Gartner? Will he be ready
o take his uncle's seat in Commons? Or should we
cast about for another candidate?"

"Far too young and irresponsible," Lord Hawksley
said, shaking his head. "We need a reliable man there.
Someone like Joshua Rawlings, or perhaps Harold
Forsythe could be persuaded to leave his position at the
reasury."

Stephen let the words wash over him, and as Lord
Hawksley debated the merits of the various candidates,
Stephen focused on his own dilemma. He could not
continue with things as they were. He needed to find
some way to connect with Diana, to prove to her that
he was the one gentleman who could make her happy.
And his brother be damned.

* * *

The more Diana thought, the more she was puzzled by George Wright's behavior. For someone she had once thought a villain, he was working very hard to win his way back into her graces. He seemed sincerely repentant, but having trusted his good nature once, she was reluctant to make the same mistake again.

She longed to discuss this with someone who knew him, but Stephen, who should have been the logical choice, had his own prejudices and was hardly a neutral observer. Finally, one afternoon as she was strolling in Hyde Park with Miss Charlotte Fox, she took the opportunity to sound her out.

"Mr. Wright is good friends with your brother, is he not?" Diana began.

"Yes," Charlotte replied. "Or rather, they were good friends, and then this spring I think they quarreled, for Arthur was to accompany Mr. Wright to France, and then at the eleventh hour Arthur changed his mind. He would not tell me why, but hinted it was some scandal. When Mr. Wright returned to London, Arthur would hardly speak with him. But then he invited him to the picnic the other day, so I suppose they have mended their disagreement."

Charlotte twirled her parasol, her eyes glancing idly over toward the banks of the Serpentine where Arthur Fox and two of his friends were deep in conversation with the Misses Binghams, a pair of twin sisters who had captivated London with their identical beauty.

"I know little of George Wright," Diana said, and never had she spoken truer words. For all that she had early been ruined by him, she could not claim to know his essential character. "But I can tell that he and his brother are not close, and I will admit that I am curious as to the cause."

Charlotte shrugged. "Families are always quarreling over one thing or another," she said. "There are times when Arthur and I can hardly bear to be in the same room as one another. But underneath it all we love one another, and if I ever needed him, I know I can count on him as a brother and as a friend."

Interesting, but hardly helpful. "And what is your impression of Mr. Wright? Is he a friend, as well? A good man, do you think?"

Charlotte's steps slowed. "His manners are pretty, and he makes an amusing companion," she said thoughtfully. "But there is something about him that I do not like. At times I think he is laughing at me, and at all of society."

"He has little patience for fools," Diana said. "Though if that is a character flaw, I must own it is mine as well."

"It is not that. Let us say rather that while I would not mind him as a dinner partner, I would be very careful about accepting an invitation to take a stroll with him alone in a moonlit garden. Of course, now that I am engaged to Lord Wiggams, the question is moot."

Diana winced and hoped her face did not show her distress. If only she had heard these words two months before, how very differently things might have turned out.

"I think you were wise to be cautious," Diana said.

"Now tell me, how are the wedding preparations advancing? Have you selected a date yet?"

Charlotte gracefully accepted the change of topic and spent a full quarter hour describing the elaborate plans for the wedding that was to take place next spring. All Diana had to do was smile and make the occasional murmur of interest. But even as she listened, she kept pondering the mystery that was the Wright brothers. Surely, somewhere, there was a key that would let her understand their behavior and the conflicting accounts that she had heard. Diana simply had to be patient and persevere.

Thirteen

The weather had been rainy with dark, gloomy skies, which perfectly suited Lord Endicott's mood. But on Thursday, the skies cleared, and with the return of the sun, he felt his own spirits begin to lift. Perhaps the situation was not as hopeless as he had feared. Finding himself at loose ends, he readily accepted Tony Dunne's invitation to join him in Hyde Park, taking advantage of the fine day to exercise their horses.

"So how goes your courtship?" Tony Dunne asked.

"Slowly," Stephen said. "Diana still hasn't forgiven me for quarreling with her. I sent her an invitation asking her to take a drive with me today, but she snubbed me. Wrote that she was already engaged."

"So I am your second choice of companion," Tony said. "It is good to know where I stand."

"I mean no insult—"

"None taken," Tony said quickly. "Only a fool would prefer an outing with an old friend to a chance to escort a pretty girl around the town."

Diana's rejection of him had rankled, and he thought longingly of those first days in London. Then he had had her all to himself. Now he had to share her time with the myriad of acquaintances that she had formed.

Not that he begrudged her enjoyment; he would not be so petty. But sometimes he wondered whether she still wanted his friendship, now that she no longer needed his support. And how could he court her if she would not even accept his invitations?

"Diana was engaged to luncheon with Miss Fox, and then they planned to spend the afternoon strolling in the park. Miss Fox fancies herself an artist and wished to sketch the river, I believe," Stephen said. He had learned of her plans when he called upon the house at Chesterfield Hill this morning, only to discover that Diana had already departed for the day.

"So that is the reason we are here, instead of in St. James's Park," Tony said, referring to their more usual ride.

"Yes," Stephen said. "I do not like how much time she is spending with Miss Fox."

"The young lady seems unexceptionable."

"I have no quarrel with her. But where one finds Miss Fox, one also finds her brother, Arthur Fox. And his role in the events of this past April is one that I am not yet ready to forgive."

As they rode along the bridle path, Stephen's eyes scanned the crowds, but he could not spot Miss Somerville among any of the small knots of strollers, nor was she one of those picnicking under the trees. Perhaps they had changed their plans, or perhaps they had already been here and left.

They rode in silence for a few moments, until the path took them down near the bank of the Serpentine Lake.

"I say, isn't that Miss Somerville? In the blue rowboat, just past that point of land?"

Stephen reined in his horse and looked; but the rowboat was turning away, so all he could see was the back of a young lady. She wore a green dress, and a straw bonnet covered her hair, giving no hint of the color underneath. But he recognized the other passenger quite clearly as Arthur Fox.

"It may be her," Stephen said. He gave a soft cluck, and his horse obediently started down the hillside toward the water. After a moment, he heard Tony Dunne following him.

The boat finished turning, and, indeed, he could see it was Miss Somerville. And the reason for the odd maneuvers became clear as well, for it was Miss Somerville who held the oars in her hands and not her escort.

The young man gestured with his arms and appeared to be instructing her. Slowly the boat righted itself and began an erratic course toward the dock. When they were just a few yards from shore, Mr. Fox looked up and saw him. He must have said something to Miss Somerville, for she turned around in her seat.

Stephen waved at her. She smiled and began to wave back. She called out something that he could not hear. Then she began to stand up.

"No!" he exclaimed, but it was already too late.

The rowboat rocked, leaning toward the left. Diana and Mr. Fox both leaned violently to the right side, with the inevitable results. There was a loud splash as the two fell into the water, and the rowboat overturned beside them.

Stephen dismounted and handed the reins to Tony Dunne. He reached the water's edge just as Diana stood up, and then Arthur Fox, leaning heavily on the rowboat, was able to stand up as well. It was fortunate that the lake was shallow after the long summer drought, for the water came only up to her thighs.

Diana gave one look at the rowboat and the hapless Arthur Fox and then began making her way toward shore. Stephen, heedless of his own clothes, jumped into the water, and walked out to meet her.

"Give me your arm," he said.

She did so, and they slogged through the muddy water and thick reeds to the bank, where Tony Dunne reached over and helped her climb up and then reached down to give Stephen a hand as well.

Stephen glanced back and saw that Arthur Fox had managed to right the boat, and with the help of another group of rowers, he was towing it in to the shore. Satisfied that the young man was in no danger, he turned to Diana.

Her dress, which had been pink, was now soaked through with muddy river water and clung to her like a second skin, revealing a generous set of curves that would make any man's mouth water. Stephen quickly stripped off his jacket and placed it around her shoulders. Despite the summer heat, she was already beginning to shiver.

"This is all your fault," Diana said.

"My fault?"

"Yes," she said, her blue eyes flashing. "Mr. Fox was teaching me to row. I was doing just fine until you distracted me."

"I was not the one who decided to try and stand up in a rowboat," Stephen pointed out. "Did he not warn you that it was unstable? What were you thinking?"

"I was not thinking," Diana said. "I was happy to see you, and look where that got me."

Her words cut him to the quick. "It was an accident," he temporized. "Now we must get you home, so you can change out of those wet clothes before you catch your death."

And before anyone else had the chance to gawk at her. They had already drawn quite a crowd of onlookers, amazed that someone could overturn a rowboat on a lake that was as calm as a millpond.

"Tony, will you—"

"I will see that your horse is returned to the stables," Tony Dunne said, reading his mind. "It is not far from here to the gate, and you can hail a hackney coach from there."

"Thank you," Stephen said.

"My pleasure. Miss Somerville, I hope we next meet under more fortunate circumstances," Tony Dunne said, tipping his hat. "And, Stephen, I advise you to take care of your lady."

"I will," he promised. Even if she did not realize it, it was clear that Miss Somerville needed protecting, from herself most of all.

When Diana returned home, a servant informed her that her father wished to speak with her. Summoning her maid, she hastily disrobed and washed off the traces of the smelly lake water. Her dress and slippers were ruined, and as for Lord Endicott's coat, it would never be the same. Even her hair was filled with mud and weeds, as she discovered when she began to brush it out. She must have looked a sight and was mortified that Lord Endicott, of all people, had seen her disgrace.

She did not know what had happened. She knew better than to move suddenly in a rowboat. Her reading had taught her that they were chancy craft, their small size making them inherently unstable. But she had been doing well, even managing to row a steady course. Then she had seen Lord Endicott, and the next thing she knew, she was in the water, scrambling for her footing.

She had felt utterly humiliated and snapped at Lord Endicott when he had presumed to scold her. Fortunately he had sensed her ill temper, and the journey home had been peaceable, if silent. She had invited him inside, but predictably he had declined, preferring to return to his own residence so he could change.

It took nearly an hour to make herself presentable, but by that time she had calmed down and was able to greet her father with equanimity.

"Papa, you wished to see me?" she asked.

Her father looked up from his book, and then marked his place with a ribbon and set it aside. She crossed the room and kissed him on the cheek in greeting.

"Diana, we need to talk," he said.

His serious expression told her that this was no light conversation that he intended. Diana sat down on the edge of a stiff-backed chair, feeling suddenly as if she were Emily's age.

"What is it? Is there something wrong?" Was it her mother? Something at home? Her sisters?

"Perhaps you should tell me," he said. He gave her a meaningful look, the one that always made her feel obscurely guilty.

"I am sorry, but it was not my fault. I do not know how the boat managed to overturn—"

"What boat?" he asked, his eyebrows raised until they nearly disappeared under his hairline.

"The rowboat this afternoon. Arthur Fox and I were out on the Serpentine Lake, when we had a mishap of sorts."

Her father shook his head. "I had not heard of this," he said.

Diana bit her tongue as she realized that there had been no need for her hasty confession. If she had only held her tongue, he might never have learned of this escapade. Then again, discovery might have been inevitable. Her father had always had a way of finding out when one of his daughters was in a scrape, especially when his eldest was involved.

"Let me guess. You were pretending that you were rowing in India where you were attacked by vicious crocodiles," her father said disapprovingly.

"Papa, I am not a child to be playing games," Diana said, very much on her dignity. Such might have been true a few years ago, but now she was a grown woman.

"Then, how did the boat overturn?"

She cast her mind back. It had all happened so quickly.

"I turned to wave to a friend on the bank. The boat rocked a little, but we would have been fine had not Mr. Fox lunged to the other side to try and compensate. It must have been his movement that tipped us over," Diana said.

In hindsight, it seemed clear that Mr. Fox was not nearly the expert in boats that he had claimed to be when she had asked him to teach her. Surely an expert would have been able to prevent their unfortunate capsizing.

"I see," her father said, closing his eyes briefly. He wore the expression of long-suffering patience that he often had when dealing with Diana and her sisters.

"But that is not why I wanted to see you," her father said. "I have heard reports that have disturbed me. Reports that you have been seen keeping company with Lord Endicott's brother."

"He has a name. George Wright," Diana said.

"Forgive me if I do not care to speak his name," her father said. "I cannot forget that he tried his best to ruin my eldest daughter. Though you seem to have forgotten that fact."

Diana felt herself flushing. "I have not forgotten," she said.

"But you have been seeing him?"

"Yes." Even admitting as much made her feel guilty. Her father let the silence stretch between them.

"He was a guest at a picnic I attended, though I did not know beforehand that he was to be there," Diana said.

"And was that the only time you saw him?"

Her father had always been good at reading the truth

in her. "No. I encountered him the other day at Hatchard's, and he insisted on taking me to Gunther's for ices."

"You went with him for ices," her father repeated. "A man who tried to rape you."

Put that way, her actions sounded ridiculous.

"I did not know how to refuse him without making a public spectacle of myself. And Mr. Wright has apologized repeatedly for his sins. I am convinced that he feels sincere regret," Diana explained.

"You misjudged him once, are you certain that you now have the measure of his character?"

It was a good question, and one that had occupied her mind for many days.

"No," Diana said. "But our encounters have been purely by chance. I have no plans to seek out his company."

Her father sighed and rubbed one hand over his face. "I swear I age a year for every month that we spend in this damn city. I will not rest easy until we are back home in Kent, where I know my neighbors, and they know us."

Diana felt guilty as she realized the strain the season was exerting upon him. He had not complained once, and yet she knew how much he disliked London. And how much more he disliked pretense in any form. It must be galling for him to have to play the part that she had assigned to him.

"Do you wish to leave?" Diana asked. "I know Mama misses the girls dreadfully."

He shook his head. "No, we said we will stay

through July, and there is no sense in changing our plans."

She felt relieved, for she did not want to leave, not when there was so much gaiety planned for the next weeks as the city gave itself over to celebrating the triumph at Waterloo. And at the same time she felt guilty for keeping her father here for her own selfish reasons.

In truth, the celebrations were only one reason that she wished to stay. Once she returned to Kent, it was highly unlikely that she would ever see Mr. Wright or his brother, Lord Endicott, again. Thus she did not want to leave, not until she had made up her mind about the brothers. Both of them offered friendship and hinted at stronger feelings, but she could not make up her mind about either of them. Was George truly a villain? Was Stephen playing the part that honor demanded, or were his affections truly engaged? She could not leave London until she knew the answers to these questions.

"If I thought you would listen, I would forbid you to ever speak with Mr. Wright again," her father said. "But I know such an order is only likely to provoke you to contrariness."

"I will promise not to seek him out," Diana said. "And if he speaks to me, I will be polite. Nothing more."

"That is as much as I can hope for. And, Diana, be very careful. You are playing with fire. Lord Endicott does not strike me as a man who will let himself be made a fool of. You need to be very certain that you know what it is you want. If you are trying to attract

Lord Endicott's attention, you are going about this the wrong way."

"I am not doing anything of the sort," Diana replied. "And as for Lord Endicott, I want nothing from him but his friendship."

It was a half-truth at best; but it seemed to satisfy her father, and Diana made her escape, grateful that she had gotten off so lightly.

Later in the quiet of her own chambers, Diana reflected upon her father's advice. It was not fair. Everyone seemed to know how she should act. Lady Endicott, Miss Charlotte Fox, her father, even Stephen felt they had a right to dictate her behavior. Lady Endicott asked for her help and obliquely warned her that Stephen was a tyrant. Miss Fox told her that George was pleasant, but not to be trusted. Her father and Stephen both lectured her on the need for appearances and on the folly of associating with George Wright. They did not care that he had apologized and offered to make amends. It seemed that no matter what George did, they would never forgive him.

They treated her as if she were a child. Everyone told her what to do, but there was no one to talk with about how she felt. She wished suddenly for her sister Mary. Mary, at least, would listen and sympathize with her dilemma.

But she already knew what Mary would say. Mary would tell her to trust her heart. But her heart had already led her astray once. This time she would make no decisions until both her heart and intellect were in agreement.

Fourteen

"I told you to stay away from her," Lord Endicott said.

He regretted the words as soon as they left his mouth. This meeting was at his request, after all, and he would be ill-served if George chose to leave before Stephen had a chance to make his point.

George brushed a speck of imaginary dust off the tassel of his boot. "I recall no such request," he said. He raised his eyes and met Stephen's gaze full on. "You asked that I conduct myself with civility, and I have done so."

Stephen took a deep breath and reminded himself that he needed to stay calm. It had taken days for George to agree to see him. The delay had only fueled Stephen's anger, for he was not used to begging anyone for favors. But for Miss Somerville's sake, he was willing to do this, and more.

They sat in the study at Grosvenor Square, which had changed little in the seven years since his father's death. The massive mahogany desk and chair gleamed under coats of beeswax polish, while his father's ivory and silver writing set sat precisely in the center of the green felt blotter. The shelves of the east wall were filled with leather-bound volumes, whose precise arrangements hinted that they were seldom if ever taken down and read. Stephen's own books were in Chesterfield Hall, and he doubted very much that George had cracked open a book since his school days.

The two brothers sat in upholstered chairs that flanked a bay window offering a view of the street and square beyond. It was a pleasant spot for conversation or whiling away idle hours with one's intimates. But even as Stephen cast his mind back, he could not ever recall a time when he and George had simply relaxed and spent an hour as friends. There was at once too much and too little between them for that kind of casual connection.

"Have you reconsidered my offer?" Stephen asked. "A thousand pounds, and I will clear your debts in London, once you resume your travels."

It was a generous offer, and George should have jumped at it. London in the season was an expensive place to be, and with his quarterly allowance pledged to pay old debts, George must be teetering on the edge of financial ruin.

"Intriguing, but you may save your generosity for someone else," George said. "I find London quite suits my mood at the moment."

He rose and crossed to the sideboard, pouring himself a generous glass of his brother's brandy. He turned and raised one eyebrow. "Brother?"

"No," Stephen replied. He was in no mood for drinking.

He wondered if he should double his offer. Or treble it. But somehow he doubted that it would have any effect. George was obviously enjoying having the upper hand over his brother for once and showed no signs that he was willing to give up his advantage.

George slowly strolled around the room, the brandy glass in his left hand, his fingers trailing along the bookshelves. "This library was all for show, you know," he commented. "Father bought the books because he thought they would look well in this room, and all gentlemen were expected to have a library. I doubt he read a dozen in his life."

"Actually, Father was a great reader," Stephen corrected him. "He gave me his own set of Virgil when I went to Eton."

"That may have been true, once," George said. "But the father I knew had far more interesting diversions to occupy his time than mere books."

Stephen tasted bile at this casual reminder of how close George had been to their father. In those last years it had been just the three of them, Caroline, George, and his father, while Stephen had been banished outside the family circle. To be certain they had dressed it up prettily enough. Soon after George's birth Stephen had been sent away to school, while his father doted over his infant son. He had returned home for summers and school breaks, but somehow his stepmother, Caroline, always made him feel as if he were the outsider, intruding upon the happy family that they had made. As George grew, he followed his mother's example, despising his older brother and taking every opportunity to cast Stephen in a bad light. Stephen's overtures of friendship were harshly rebuffed, until he learned to perfect a mask of indifference.

His father had always seemed oblivious to the tensions that ran between his two sons. Or perhaps he had merely ignored them, avoiding unpleasantness as was his habit. Why else would he have given Stephen sole use of the house on Chesterfield Hill when Stephen was barely twenty? His peers had envied him his freedom, not realizing that this freedom came with a bitter price.

Stephen searched within himself. Surely there ought to be some scrap of affection for George, of brotherly feeling. After all, their father's blood ran through both their veins. But, instead, Stephen looked at George and he felt nothing except contempt. It was as if he gazed upon the face of a stranger.

He watched as George perched himself on the desk, idly swinging one foot.

"In a way I suppose you are like these books. Dull and virtuous and precisely what one expects to find in such a setting. It is no wonder that Miss Somerville prefers my company to yours."

Stephen rose to his feet. "I do not want you to speak of her."

"Then, why else am I here? And you cannot deny it is the truth. After all, she is hardly shunning me, is she? Chatting with me at the opera, meeting at the park for an afternoon picnic, ices at Gunther's. It is all of a piece, is it not?"

His mind whirled. A picnic? Ices at Gunther's tea shop? This was the first he had heard of such excursions. And yet why would George lie? It would be all too easy for Stephen to confirm the truth.

His mind brought forth images of Diana laughing;

only this time he saw George standing beside her. George, whom she ought to despise but, instead, seemed to have forgiven.

"You will stay away from her," Stephen repeated.

"Or?"

"Or I will forget I am a gentleman and do the unexpected," he said, his voice soft with menace.

George raised his brandy glass to his lips and drained it in a single swallow. He set the glass down on the gleaming desk top and then pushed himself off onto his feet. "I believe you might," he said. "You love her, don't you?"

"That is none of your affair," Stephen replied, wary of handing his brother yet another weapon that could be used against him.

George nodded, as if his brother's words had confirmed his belief.

"I will keep my distance," he said. "Though I can make no promises for Miss Somerville's behavior."

It was the best he could hope for.

George strode to the door and opened it. Then he paused, resting one hand on the doorframe. "You know, in a way you should thank me," he said.

"How so?"

"Without me, you would never have had a chance at a woman like Miss Somerville. She craves excitement and adventure in her life and wanted a gentleman who could satisfy her needs. But thanks to my meddling, she is forced to settle for what she can get. Forced to settle for you."

Stephen growled and moved toward his brother, but George darted through the doorway. As Stephen reached the hall, he saw his brother disappearing down the staircase, stepping around two housemaids who were polishing the floor.

A part of him wanted to follow and to settle his differences with his brother once and for all. Regardless of watching eyes or the scandal it would no doubt bring. But another part of him, the cautious part that ruled his nature, slowed his feet.

There was nothing to be gained from a confrontation with his brother. George had given his promise to stay away from Diana, and now it remained to be seen if he intended to keep to his word.

Stephen returned to the study with a heavy heart and sat down in the chair that he still thought of as his father's. With the fingers of his right hand he traced idle designs on the blotter as he thought about his predicament. There was nothing more he could do. George had resisted bribes, threats, and an appeal to his so-called good nature. The best he could hope for now was that George would find some other diversion to keep him entertained for the next few weeks.

After all, as far as George knew, the engagement was real. No doubt he envisioned a lifetime of being able to torment his older brother.

But Stephen knew otherwise. In a few short weeks Miss Somerville would leave London, and then she would leave his life. If he wanted her to stay with him, he would have to convince her that he was the better of the two brothers. The only one who could give her the love that she deserved.

* * *

It took three full days for Diana to forgive Lord Endicott for having borne witness to the mishap at the Serpentine Lake. She knew it was petty of her, but somehow she felt as if he were to blame, if not for the boat overturning, then certainly for having stayed there to bear witness to her disgrace.

Knowing that she was once again the subject of London gossip was also unpleasant, and Diana was forced to grit her teeth as guests at Lady Knowlton's rout kept coming up to her, inquiring about her sudden desire to go swimming in the lake. Even her friends could not resist poking gentle fun at her, and she reluctantly conceded that it must have been an amusing sight. To everyone except the participants, that was.

But after a few days she calmed down and wrote to Lord Endicott, inviting him to take tea with her and her parents on the next afternoon. He accepted with eagerness, and on that afternoon she dressed with special care, remembering her bedraggled appearance the last time he saw her.

When she entered the drawing room, Stephen rose to greet her. "Miss Somerville, you look lovely as always," he said.

She searched his face, but found no hint of mockery.

"I seem to recall when last we met that I looked more like a drowned rat," Diana said. "And I must thank you for your kindness in seeing me home so swiftly."

"I am grateful you suffered no ill effects from your dunking," Stephen answered. "And as for your appearance, the details have faded in my mind, as I trust you have forgotten my own dishevelment."

"I would prefer to forget the whole day entirely," Diana said. "As, I am sure, would Mr. Fox."

"Have you sworn off boating for life?"

"No," Diana said, after a moment's reflection. It was a skill that could prove useful, after all. Even in England there were lakes and ponds aplenty, and one never knew when a knowledge of rowing might be needed. "I would still like to learn, but next time I will be more careful whom I choose to teach me."

"It is wise to find the best teacher one can," Stephen agreed. "And rowboats of the type you were in the other day are quite tricky. You might do better to start on a punt, in a quiet lake where there are fewer distractions."

"Are you offering yourself as an instructor?"

Stephen shrugged. "Perhaps. There are no suitable lakes near London, but at our estate in Eastbourne there is a large pond, and a boathouse. As a boy I enjoyed many hours upon the pond."

"It must have been lovely," Diana replied.

She wondered if there was another meaning behind his words. Was he hinting that he wished to spend more time with her? Was this an oblique invitation to visit his home? Or had he simply fallen into the pattern of pretending to others that he and Diana had a future together that now he said such things without thinking?

She wished to question him further, but just then her parents arrived, along with the tea cart. They exchanged greetings, and then Stephen inquired about her sisters back in Kent. Her mother, launched into her favorite topic, insisted on reading aloud the latest letter from home, in which all six sisters had felt a need to share their latest news. The conversation then turned general. Diana enjoyed herself and marveled at how comfortable Stephen seemed to be in this family gathering. He was equally at ease listening to her mother's doting accounts of the girls as he was in arguing politics with her father. When he finally rose, she was startled at how swiftly time had passed.

Before taking his leave, he invited Diana to join him on an excursion tomorrow, promising to show her a special treat. With eagerness she agreed.

Fifteen

Diana held Lord Endicott's arm firmly as he steered her through the crowds that thronged Green Park. From all sides they were pressed in as gentry and commoners alike filled every square foot of open ground, enjoying the warm sunshine and festival atmosphere. On their left she saw an enterprising fiddler playing a lively tune while a small boy carried a basket among the spectators. A few yards away two tumblers performed acrobatic somersaults. They briefly caught her eye, but then she remembered the reason why she and Lord Endicott had come here and pressed onward.

She twisted her head from side to side and then sighed in frustration. "Can you see it?" she asked.

"Not yet," Lord Endicott said. "I believe they were to set up on the north field. Past that stand of trees, over there." He pointed the way with his walking stick.

She tugged his arm, urging him to greater speed. He smiled indulgently and increased his pace. They followed a well-trodden path up a slight rise and through the trees, and then suddenly, there it was.

Before her the crowd gathered around a great balloon, which though tethered to the ground, seemed ready to soar to the heavens. The balloon itself was made of alternating panels of green and yellow silks, festooned with red, white, and blue buntings that gave it a most patriotic appearance. Underneath the silken canopy, she could make out glimpses of a wicker basket and a half dozen men busy at various incomprehensible tasks.

"It is just as wonderful as I imagined," she declared.

"Would you like to see it closer?"

Diana nodded. The crowd around the balloon was thick, but with persistent politeness, the viscount was able to make their way through until they stood close enough to hear the aeronaut, Mr. Poundstone, expound upon his creation.

"Now this here balloon is a vast improvement over the French design. The burners have been redesigned, allowing safer control of the inflation process, which makes the balloon able to fly," he said, gesturing with his left arm.

At his cue, his assistant turned a lever, and a jet of flame shot upward. The crowed *oohed,* and Mr. Poundstone nodded, as if he had just accomplished a spectacular feat. Then, at his command, the assistant extinguished the jet, and Mr. Poundstone continued his lecture.

"I myself have traveled great distances in this very balloon, often fifty miles or more, in perfect safety and comfort," Mr. Poundstone testified. "And in fair weather, and with the right winds, an intrepid man might cross the English Channel in this very vessel."

"The Channel," Diana echoed. What a marvelous feat that would be. Such an explorer would, indeed, be celebrated, and if it were a woman who made the trip. . . .

"I hope he knows how to swim," Stephen added, sotto voce.

Diana nudged him with her elbow. No doubt Stephen would never undertake such a journey. Or if he did, he would have made arrangements to be followed at all times by a sailing vessel, in case of mishap or danger. Perhaps even two sailing vessels, to suit his cautious nature.

Not that she blamed him. It was not his fault if he lacked a spirit of adventure.

She listened as Mr. Poundstone continued to expound upon the glories of his craft and the new worlds that these brave aeronauts were opening up. When the explorer finished his lecture, she applauded enthusiastically with the rest.

"Thank you," she said, turning to Stephen. "This was a lovely treat."

She knew she was beaming ear to ear and was not surprised when Stephen grinned back at her.

"It was my pleasure," he replied.

Diana knew she looked foolish, but she could not help smiling. She had always wanted to see a hot air balloon up close, and it had seemed a dream come true when Lord Endicott had called and offered to be her escort.

She was happy, she realized. And it was not just the excursion. She was happy because he was here. For she had missed this. Missed the connection she had formed with Lord Endicott. It seemed ages since they had been allowed to simply enjoy the pleasure of each other's company. She had not felt so free since George had returned. But as quickly as his name came to mind, she banished it. She would not ruin this day by thinking of George and the confusing emotions he stirred within her.

"The crowd is thinning. Perhaps we can exchange a few words with Mr. Poundstone," Diana said.

Stephen allowed himself to be led over and then waited until the aeronaut caught sight of his fashionably dressed spectators.

"My lord, I am at your service," he said, giving a short bow.

Up close the aeronaut was older than she had expected, with a ruddy complexion and a rotund figure. *Perhaps he acts as his own ballast,* Diana thought, and then bit her lip.

"I am Lord Endicott, and this is my fiancée, Miss Somerville," Stephen said.

"Lord Endicott. Miss Somerville," Mr. Poundstone repeated, bowing to each of them.

"Miss Somerville was most impressed with your lecture," Lord Endicott said.

"Indeed, I was," Diana interjected. "Tell me, do you plan to make any ascents in the near future? Today, perhaps?"

Seeing the balloon on the ground was fascinating, but now she wished to witness the spectacle of watching the craft soar into the sky above their heads.

To her disappointment, Mr. Poundstone shook his head. "I am afraid not, miss. The winds today are too strong, and from the southwest, which is a bad omen for flight. We hope to do better on the morrow."

"Of course," Diana said. Apparently ships that sailed the air were governed by the same rules as ships that sailed the sea. Both must comply with the vagaries of the wind and weather.

She wondered if she could persuade Stephen to bring her back tomorrow to see the launch.

"Of course, we will be doing a tethered ascent, for those that wish," Mr. Poundstone added.

"No," Stephen said.

Diana ignored him.

"A tethered ascent?" she asked.

"Yes, you see these ropes?" Mr. Poundstone gestured to the heavy ropes that were fastened to brass rings on each of the four sides of the basket. "We can launch the balloon and ascend safely to a height of over four hundred feet, and then be lowered gently back to earth. Gives folks a taste of ballooning as it were."

"Stephen—" Diana began.

"No," he repeated. His jaw was set, and he tugged at her arm.

But she was immovable.

"For a modest fee, of course," Mr. Poundstone said. "A mere one hundred pounds, and yourself and the gentle lady here can witness the spectacle of London as seen from the air."

Diana's heart began to race.

"No," Stephen repeated. "It is not safe. And it is certainly not fit for a lady."

"It is perfectly safe," Diana retorted. "Those are good stout ropes, see?"

"The finest ropes in all of England. Even the Royal Navy has none better," one of the assistants interjected.

Stephen glared at the man, who wisely retreated to the opposite side of the balloon.

"It would be a scandal," he said.

She knew he was weakening.

"Nonsense," Diana said firmly. "Women have been aeronauts since the invention of the balloon. Think of Mrs. Tible and Mrs. Sage. They flew over thirty years ago, real flights, not a tame tethered excursion. And just this winter Mademoiselle Garnerin astonished London by ascending in a balloon and then descending by a parachute to the ground below."

Stephen closed his eyes, and she could see him swallow. "I saw her performance," he said.

"You did? Was she magnificent?"

"Brave. But I have no wish to be her husband."

She blinked at the change of subject. "I do not see where that has anything to do with this. I do not wish to be a parachutist. All I wish for is a simple ascent."

Stephen shook his head.

"Come now, miss, don't pout. If he won't take you, I will," someone called from the crowd.

"Listen to your husband," a matronly older woman advised. "He knows what is right."

Diana ignored the shouted advice, which gradually grew louder as those around them joined in to offer their conflicting opinions.

There were a few catcalls, and she knew that they would have to take their leave soon, before they became the center of a disturbance.

This was all Stephen's fault, she decided crossly.

This was a once in a lifetime chance for her to live her dream of being an adventurer, and he was ruining it for her with his cautious nature.

"I should have known you were the wrong man for this excursion," she said coldly. "You have absolutely no sense of adventure."

She caught a glimpse of pain, quickly hidden, and knew she had gone too far. But before she could apologize, he turned to Mr. Poundstone.

"We would like to take you up on your generous offer," he said. "At once."

Stephen felt a strange lurch, and then the basket began to gently sway as they began their ascent. He did not know how this had happened. At one moment he had been basking in Miss Somerville's enjoyment of the day, congratulating himself on having found something that would please her so well. And then, before he quite knew what was happening, he had agreed to this insane stunt.

Mr. Poundstone and his assistants had rushed through their preparations, perhaps sensing that if they delayed, Stephen would change his mind. The balloon was already inflated, so all that remained was one final cycle of the burners to heat the gas, and then he found himself helping Miss Somerville climb into the narrow wicker basket, before he took his own place beside her. Mr. Poundstone stood on the opposite side of the basket, the now unlit burner between them. A few strategically placed sandbags for ballast ensured that the basket remained level as they rose.

Every instinct in him screamed that this was folly. It was reckless, possibly even dangerous. And even if the ascension went without a hitch, this escapade would only add to Miss Somerville's reputation as an eccentric, someone who flouted the rules of ordinary society.

But none of that mattered to him. Not when faced with the terrible disappointment he had seen in Diana's eyes when she had deplored his refusal. She had declared him the wrong man for this excursion, and in her words he heard what she had not said. He was the wrong man for her, too dull for her tastes. It was no wonder she had sought out George's company.

And so he had agreed to this insanity, desperate to prove that he was not the dull stick that she thought him to be. But even as he put his arm around her waist to steady her, he was having second thoughts.

"Is this not marvelous?" Diana asked, craning her neck around as she tried to see everything at once. "Look, we are already level with the tree tops."

There was a sudden jerk, and the basket tilted to the left. Diana gasped. Stephen tightened his grasp on the railing, ensuring that Diana remained within the circle of his right arm.

Mr. Poundstone leaned over the side of the basket. "Mind the ropes, you damn fools," he called down. Then he straightened up. "Er, begging your pardon, miss."

The basket righted itself and began to rise again. Stephen fought the urge to demand that they return to the ground at once. Such an action would be certain to antagonize Diana, and should she feel thwarted, she would just find someone else to accompany her next time. Someone like his brother, George. Some fool who did not care for her and would stand idly by while she risked her life. An image sprang to him of Diana, standing on the basket railing as she prepared to jump out and descend by parachute.

He closed his eyes, swallowing hard to banish the awful image.

"Are you feeling well?" Diana asked.

He opened his eyes.

"If you are not well, there is no need to go higher. We can descend," she offered generously.

Her kindness warmed his heart, for it was proof that she did, indeed, care for him. But he would not take the cowardly route of using her concern for him to force her to curtail her adventure. They had committed themselves now, and they might as well make the most of this experience, for he had no intention of doing this again. Ever.

"It is nothing," he said.

Their ascent slowed, until the ropes were stretched taught, and they came to a halt. The balloon and its cargo swayed gently in the winds, rocking much as a boat would upon the waves. After a few moments he became used to the motion and was able to relax his grip on the basket.

"See? There is St. James's and the palace. And to the south, along the river is Westminster Abbey. And that must be the Admiralty House, for you can see the signal towers on the roof," he said, pointing with his left arm.

"If you follow the river, you can see the Houses of Parliament and the tower bridge, of course. And if you turn your attention to the northeast, you can see the great dome of St. Paul's," Mr. Poundstone said, taking over the narration.

As they slowly turned, he could see nearly the whole of London laid out below their feet. The crowded park seemed far smaller than he remembered, as did the surrounding streets. But the great monuments were even more impressive from the air, allowing one to glimpse their true size as they dominated their surroundings.

He wondered what it would be like if they ascended higher. Would they be able to see more? Or would there come a point where the details would blur into unrecognizability? And what if they were actually to cut free of the restraining ropes and to fly across the city? Such vistas would, indeed, be amazing.

He began to see why Diana was so fascinated by the aeronautical craft and looked over to tell her as much.

But Diana was looking decidedly pale, her eyes fixed on the ground below.

"We are so high. And those people seem so very small, almost like toy figures," she said.

She straightened up and then pressed one hand against her forehead as all color drained from her face.

"Oh, dear," she said, and he was just in time to grasp her as she went limp in his arms.

"Take us down. Now," Stephen ordered, drawing Diana in an embrace to hold her upright.

Mr. Poundstone picked up a cloth flag and began waving it over the side of the basket. After a few moments, Stephen felt the now familiar lurch as those below began to haul in the ropes. Unlike the smoothness of their ascent, the descent was halting, as if the assistants were unused to working in unison. Still, they were making progress toward the ground, however imperceptible.

Stephen turned his attention to Diana, who remained unconscious. If he were anywhere else, he would lay her on a sofa or even the ground. But in this damn wicker monstrosity there was barely room to stand and no room to sit or lay her down.

He shook her arms gently. "Diana? Wake up," he entreated.

She moaned and began to stir, then opened her eyes. "What happened?"

"You fainted."

She shook her head. "Nonsense. I never faint," she declared.

He smiled, relieved to see that her spirits were intact. As her cheeks once again filled with rosy color, he realized that he was still holding her in an intimate embrace.

Honor dictated that he release her, now that she no longer needed his support. But, instead, driven by impulse, he bent his head and claimed her lips in a kiss.

Stephen had kissed her. And somehow that had changed everything, though she had been too dazed and confused to realize it at the time. Still dizzy from her unexpected fainting spell, she had awoken to find herself clasped against his body, his arms wrapped around her in an intimate embrace. And then, he had kissed her. Not a gentle brush of the lips, but a slow, sweet, rapturous meeting of their mouths. By the time he raised his head, she was gasping for air.

She had half expected him to apologize for taking such liberties. To explain his unconventional behavior. But he had not. Nor had he kissed her again, much to her disappointment. Instead, when the balloon had reached the ground, he had helped her alight to the cheers of the crowd. And then he had escorted her back to the gig and instructed the coachman to return them to the town house, as if this had been an ordinary outing like any other.

The streets were so noisy that it was impossible to converse during the short drive. But as they reached Chesterfield Hill, she made one last effort. "Wait," she told him. "There are matters we need to discuss."

Stephen flashed her a crooked smile. "Yes," he agreed. "But not today. We both need time."

"Time for what?" How dare he behave in such a contradictory fashion? First he embraced her, and now he was seeking to distance himself from her, in both body and heart.

"Time to converse," he said. "Which will not be today, for unless I miss my guess, those carriages outside the door mean that your mother is entertaining callers this afternoon, and you are already late."

Diana groaned as she recalled that her mother had invited a half dozen of their acquaintances to tea this afternoon, along with their daughters. They must all be wondering what had happened to delay Diana's arrival.

"Bother that. We can go elsewhere. Might as well be hung for a sheep as a lamb. I am already so late that there is no point."

But Lord Endicott would not be swayed. "No," he said. "See, our arrival has already been noticed."

And, indeed, a footman was descending the steps of the town house, ready to help her descend from the carriage.

"I will see you soon, and then we will talk," he said.

"When? Tonight? Tomorrow?"

He shook his head. "I am already engaged for tomorrow."

"You are engaged to me," she said, her temper rising.

He chuckled. "Yes, and a stubborn woman you are. Monday, then, if that suits your favor?"

"Monday it is," she agreed. That was only two days from now, though it seemed an eternity.

"It is only a brief delay," he said. It was uncanny the way he could read her mind. "And it will give us both time to think about what it is that we truly want."

"But I know what I want."

"Do you?"

The words were mild, but there was nothing mild in his searching state. It was as if he were trying to see into her soul.

Before she could respond, she felt the coach slowing, and it came to a stop in front of the town house. The door swung open, and the footman, Timothy, set down a wooden step to help her descend.

"My thanks for a lovely afternoon. I enjoyed myself greatly," Diana said. She knew her words sounded trite, but she was all too aware of their watching audience. What she had to say to Stephen she would say in private.

"As did I," he replied.

He took her hand and kissed the back of it, his eyes following her as she descended from the carriage and walked up the stairs. As she reached the door, she turned and gave a half wave. He nodded, and then at his signal, the hackney coach drove away, leaving her alone with her thoughts.

Sixteen

Diana sat in her bedroom, curled in the window seat. There was an open book in her lap, but her mind was not on the fantastic adventures of Messrs. Lewis and Clark as they explored the American wilderness in search of the legendary Northwest Passage. Instead, her mind drifted to a mystery much closer to home, the enigma of Lord Endicott and his increasingly strange behavior toward her. In the early days of their acquaintance she thought she had the full measure of his character, but these last few days had shown him to be a man of unexpected depths, one capable of surprising her.

The more she turned the puzzle over in her mind, the less satisfied she was. What had he meant when he advised her to be certain what it was that she wanted? Was he speaking of their engagement? Or was she reading into his words only what she wanted to hear?

Her frustration grew as she realized that it would be another day before she saw him. This time, she would not let him make an easy escape. Like it or not, he would stay until he had answered all her questions.

There was a scratch at the door, and she looked up to see the young housemaid, Annie. This must be her half day, for rather than wearing the ordinary blue muslin that was her normal uniform, Annie was dressed quite smartly in a printed calico dress, which Diana vaguely recognized as having been one of her castoffs.

"You look quite fine today, Annie," Diana said, wondering why the girl had not changed out of her finery before resuming her duties.

"Yes, miss. Thank you, miss," Annie said, bobbing a curtsy. "Begging your pardon, but I have a message for you. A message from a gentleman."

"Yes," Diana prompted.

"The gentleman said to tell you that he would be waiting in the green, at the end of the square. Said he needed to see you, to talk with you and the like."

Stephen. So she had not been alone in her impatience. He, too, could not wait until tomorrow. Diana's pulse quickened, and she quickly rose to her feet.

"When was this?"

"Just now, miss, as I was coming back from walking with my Frank," Annie answered. "Though I would hurry if I was you. Men being fickle, don't you know. No telling how long he'll wait."

"Thank you, Annie. You have been most helpful," Diana said.

The housemaid bobbed a curtsy and disappeared.

Diana crossed over to her dressing stand and reached for the bellpull, then hesitated. There was no time to summon her maid, nor did she wish to face the inevitable questions. Instead, she opened the wardrobe and hastily pulled out a walking dress of pink-and-white-stripped muslin. In less than a quarter hour she had changed, and after putting a straw bonnet on her head, she picked up the matching parasol.

She went downstairs. For once luck was with her, for the foyer was deserted and she was able to leave the house without being seen, or being forced to take one of the servants to play chaperone. What she had to say to Stephen she would say in private.

She hastened down the sidewalk until she reached the wrought-iron fence that surrounded the small park set aside for the enjoyment of the residents of the square. Opening the gate, she slipped inside.

There was a brick wall on one side where the garden butted up against a town house. Thick bushes acted as a perimeter on the other three sides of the garden, providing privacy and screening out the noises from the surrounding streets. Scarcely the size of the kitchen garden at home, in crowded London this garden was a lovingly tended luxury, and the beautiful flower beds drew their fair share of admirers. But this afternoon the garden was empty, save for a gentleman who stood by a cherry tree.

"Stephen," she called.

He turned, and as she recognized his face, her eager steps drew to a halt. For this was not Stephen, but rather his brother, George Wright.

Bitter disappointment welled up within her as she realized that she had allowed her hopes to lead her astray. Of course this was not Lord Endicott. The viscount would never have suggested a clandestine meeting. Nor was he the type to give in to his impatience. If he had said he would see her on Monday, then Monday it would be, regardless of personal inclinations. She had been a fool to think anything else.

George crossed the few steps that separated them. "Miss Somerville, I thank you for coming."

"I was expecting someone else," she said. She knew it was not fair, but she blamed him for her disappointment.

"And would you have come if you had known it was me?"

"No," she said honestly. Now she regretted her impulsiveness in not having brought one of the servants with her. Not that she feared for her virtue. George appeared sober enough, and she thought him no threat. But still, it was highly improper of her to meet with him in such a secluded setting.

"I know this is irregular, but I had to speak with you one last time," he said.

Despite herself, she grew curious.

"Last time?" she asked.

"Come, please," he said, indicating a nearby marble bench. Diana took a seat at one end, carefully arranging her skirts, and George took a seat at the other.

"In a few days I am to leave London," he said. "I find I can no longer bear it here. The pettiness, the hypocrisy, the tedious social rounds. I will not stay here and let them turn me into another one of their mindless drones."

"You must do as you feel best," Diana said, wondering why he felt compelled to tell her this.

"I will regret nothing of what I leave behind," George said. "Except you."

Her breath caught in her throat as he turned the full

force of his gaze on her. His eyes were open wide in apparent innocence.

"Come with me," he said. "Come with me and I will give you the world. I will show you the Continent, and when we have tired of Europe, we can see Greece and India and even Egypt if you dare. You will be the most famous female adventuress since Lady Stanhope."

"As your mistress?" Diana's voice was cold.

"No, as my wife," George said. He slipped off the bench and knelt down on the grass at her feet. "I know I do not deserve you, but I beg you to forgive me. For I love you. I could not stay away from you before, and I cannot leave England now unless you will come with me."

"My parents would never agree," Diana said.

"They have never understood you," George said. "They wish you to live a conventional life. My only wish is to make you happy."

There was truth in what he said. Her parents loved her dearly, but she knew that they did not understand her curiosity and her longing to explore more of the world than could be found in a country village.

"Come with me, and in time they will reconcile themselves to the match. Just name the day, and if we leave at dawn, we can be in Bristol by nightfall. From there we can board a ship to wherever you please and have the captain marry us."

He was offering her everything she had always wanted. A life filled with adventure and a chance to explore the world. Four months ago she would have leapt at this chance, but now she hesitated.

"What of your brother?"

"What of him? Marrying him would be a mistake He would make you miserable, a slave to duty, just as he is himself."

There was something in the expression of his eyes that made her blood run cold. And in that instant she realized that her decision was already made and, indeed, had been made some time ago.

"You must hate him very much," she said.

George blinked at her.

"Stand up," Diana said. "You look like a fool."

He rose to his feet, brushing stray blades of grass from the knees of his pantaloons.

"You may have tricked me once, but I am wiser now," Diana said. "Even if your offer was sincere, I still would not go with you."

His lips curled in scorn. "He will have no patience with your foolish whims," he said.

She was shocked at how easily he cast aside the mask of the lovesick suitor. To think that she had almost allowed herself to be taken in by him. Again. Stephen had been right to warn her about his brother. But then she had been blind, in so many ways.

"It is true that Stephen and I are quite different in temperament," Diana said. "But since the engagement is a sham, your concern is unwarranted."

"A sham?"

"A pretext," Diana said. She rose to her feet and began to pace, wishing to put some distance between her and the source of her aggravation.

"When your brother heard of my predicament, he came to offer himself in marriage," Diana explained.

"But since I had no wish to marry, we agreed to this ruse to restore my reputation. An engagement, for the remainder of the season. Once I return to Kent in the fall, I am to cry off, setting us both free."

George shook his head. "You are lying."

"Why would I lie? Ask your brother. Ask my father. Ask Tony Dunne if you like. They all know of the scheme."

"Why wasn't my mother told? When she wrote me in Belgium . . ." His voice trailed off as he realized what he had revealed.

"She summoned you home at once. Hoping your return would put a spoke in our engagement. Stephen suspected as much," Diana said.

"I could still ruin you, you know," George said. "All I have to do is hold you here until someone arrives who can bear witness to our tryst. I could then go to Stephen and tell him we have been meeting secretly for weeks now."

His threatening words were belied by the slump to his shoulders as he realized that all of his scheming had come to naught. From deep inside she found a scrap of pity for him. Poor George, so blinded by his envy and hate that he could not realize that Stephen was not the enemy. George was destroying himself with his actions, and nothing Stephen could do would change that.

"And why would he believe you over me? You lost his trust years ago. And if you wish to hurt your brother, you will have to find another target. In a few days I will leave London, and this sham engagement will be at an end," she said, willing him to believe her.

George could still stir up trouble if he had a mind, and she did not want to see Stephen hurt.

"I think you have underestimated my brother's feelings for you," George said. "He was willing to buy me off to ensure your happiness."

"And you have misjudged his patience," Diana retorted. "I think it would be wise of you to keep to your plan and leave London. His forbearance will not last forever."

To her relief he did not argue further, but, instead, with a mocking bow, he left. She watched him depart and then sank down on the bench in weariness, emotionally drained by their encounter.

In her mind she kept turning over George's final words. He had hinted that Stephen held deep feelings for her, but even if it was true, George was the last person that Stephen was likely to confide in. Perhaps George had simply been toying with her, raising false hopes that he knew would be crushed.

There was only one man who could answer her questions, and the hours until their next meeting seemed to stretch into infinity.

Monday morning dawned, and as the first rays of sunlight streamed through her windows, Diana opened her eyes. She had spent a restless night, turning over in her mind a dozen scenarios of what she would say to Lord Endicott and what he might say to her in reply. She knew what she wanted. She had realized that yesterday, and in a way she owed thanks to the despicable

George Wright, for he had forced her to acknowledge the truth of her own heart.

But what did Stephen want? What caused him to be so friendly at one moment and then so distant and forbidding at the next? He had kissed her and then had practically refused to speak with her. Did he regret their embrace? Did he resent her for bringing out his unconventional side? Was it only her wishful thinking that made her think there was true affection between them?

Her mind was filled with doubts, and she knew suddenly that she could not sit idly at home, waiting for him to call upon her. She would go to him and demand that he speak with her. This resolution made, she rose from her bed and summoned her maid to help her dress.

She left the house before either of her parents had ventured below stairs, and arrived in Grosvenor Square as the church bells began to toll the hour of eight. As the hackney coach drew up before his residence, Diana felt a sudden surge of doubt. What if Lord Endicott was not home? What if he was still sleeping?

What if he said no to her, her mind added. Then what would she do?

It was time to act, before her courage deserted her entirely. Squaring her shoulders, she descended from the carriage, followed by her maid, Jenna, who had refused to let her leave the house alone.

Lifting her skirts, she climbed the steep steps that led to the door which remained closed. She lifted the heavy brass knocker and banged it thrice.

She waited a minute, but there was no response. The

footman assigned to watch the door must be busy else-where, she realized, for only a madwoman would call at such an hour.

She banged the knocker again, harder this time. Then she heard the scrape of metal as the inner bolts were unlocked. The door swung open only a few inches.

"Tradesmen to the rear, you dolt," a male voice said.

"I am not a tradesman," Diana said.

The door opened wide, revealing a footman who eyed her insolently. She did not recognize him, but then, she had been to Grosvenor Square on only a handful of occasions.

"Leave now, and be grateful I don't call the watch on you," he said, his gaze fixed on Diana's chest. "My master has no need for a light-skirt, particularly not one so foolish as to come calling at his own home in broad daylight."

"As his fiancée, I am grateful to hear that," Diana replied. "You may tell Lord Endicott that Miss Somerville has called and wishes to speak with him. At once."

The footman's jaw dropped open, and as she ad-vanced, he automatically stepped aside, holding the door open for her and Jenna to advance.

"You will show me where I can wait," Diana said. "And after you have given my message to Lord Endi-cott, you will be kind enough to show my maid, Jenna, to the kitchen, where she can have a cup of tea while she waits."

The footman's eyes narrowed as he tried to make

sense of the situation. Then, perhaps deciding that discretion was the better part of valor, he nodded.

"Yes, miss," he said. "If you will follow me?"

He led her into a small parlor, which she recognized from her earlier visits. Then he disappeared, along with Jenna. The door had scarcely closed behind him when it opened again, revealing the figure of Lord Endicott.

He wore only a simple linen shirt tucked into a pair of buckskin trousers and a pair of well-worn slippers upon his feet. She realized that she had interrupted his toilette, and rather than waiting, he had rushed down to see her.

"Diana," he said, crossing the room and then taking her hands in his. "What is wrong? What brings you here, alone, at such an hour?"

The concern in his eyes warmed her heart and bolstered her courage which had been flagging.

"I had to see you," Diana said. "I could not wait until this afternoon. You promised me we would talk, and now is the time."

He relinquished her hands and then ran his right hand through his hair, his face reflecting his confusion. "You could not wait till this afternoon?"

"No," she said. "I am not willing to wait another hour."

"Very well," he said, gesturing to the nearby sofa. "Please have a seat and we will talk."

She sat down on the chintz sofa, and he took a seat in the chair opposite her.

Diana took a deep breath. She had practiced this speech a dozen times on the carriage ride over here, but now that she was here, the carefully rehearsed words flew out of her head. What could she say to make him understand how she felt?

"George came to see me yesterday," she began.

"I'm sorry," Stephen said. "I warned him not to bother you. I will—"

"I don't need you to do anything about George," Diana interrupted him. "I am quite capable of dealing with George myself. What I need from you is to listen."

Stephen nodded. "I am listening."

"George told me that he was leaving England and resuming his travels. He wanted me to go with him, as his wife. To lead the life of adventure that I have always dreamed of."

Stephen's whole body tensed, and she could see the muscles in his throat convulse.

"And?" he prompted.

"And I told him no," Diana said.

Stephen's body sagged almost imperceptibly in relief.

"You were wise not to trust him," he told her.

"Oh, I think he was sincere enough. In his own way."

Last night, as she had waited vainly for sleep to come, she had given the matter much thought. George's restlessness and his impatience for the conventions of society echoed her own nature, and she felt certain that his desire to travel was, indeed, sincere. And his offer of marriage was no doubt genuine. Not simply because George wished to steal her from his brother, proving once and for all who was the better man. No doubt George had also counted on Stephen's affection for her to ensure that he would provide his younger brother with a generous allowance that would allow them both to live well during their travels.

"Then, why did you refuse him?"

"Because I do not want to marry George. He is nothing but a spoiled boy, and we would make each other miserable within a fortnight," Diana said.

"So that is the end of it, then," Stephen said.

"George made me realize something about myself. Something that I have known for weeks now," Diana confessed. She looked quickly at his face and then down at her hands, which were nervously twining themselves in her lap.

"I know what I want. I do not want to marry George, nor do I wish to be a famous adventuress. Not if it means leaving you. I know we entered this engagement under false pretenses, but things have changed. I want to be your bride in truth, if you will have me."

"Are you certain this is what you want?" His voice was low, and his face was full of doubts.

"Of course," she said tartly. "Why else would I have come here at such an uncivilized hour? I love you, you fool."

Her words brought a faint smile to his face, and she felt her nervousness begin to ease.

"Even though I am thoroughly conventional and predictable and not at all likely to take you exploring along the Amazonian rivers?"

"Of course. Because you are also honorable and kind, and you understand me even if you do not always agree with me. And no other man has made me feel the way you do when you kiss me," Diana said, her cheeks flushing.

Stephen rose to his feet, and taking her hands in his, he raised her up so they stood together. "I love you, too, Diana," he said. "I have wanted to say that for weeks now, ever since the night of our engagement ball. But I feared driving you away, for I knew you would never settle for a dull stick like myself."

"You value yourself too little," Diana said.

"Then, it is good that I will have you around to remind me of my worth," he answered.

"I cannot change who I am," Diana said, needing her own reassurance. "Are you truly ready to be married to a madcap eccentric? A woman who inveigles you to ride in hot air balloons and who knows what other folly? We will be the talk of London. Again."

"I do not want you to change," Stephen said. "And as for gossip, as long as they are speaking about the two of us, I do not care what they have to say. Let us show them what a love match is meant to be."

His words banished the last of the worries from her heart, and she felt her face break into a broad smile. Greatly daring, she reached up with one hand and caressed the back of his head and then pressed her lips to his.

His lips were soft and tender upon her own. Then they parted, and the sweetness turned to fire as his tongue traced her lips and then dipped inside to explore her mouth. He gathered her to him, pressing her soft curves against every inch of his hard body. She felt herself becoming light-headed, and only his strong hold kept her from sinking to the ground.

"We can be married as soon as the banns are called," he said, when finally he lifted his head so they could breathe.

"Yes," Diana said, with the small part of her brain that was still capable of rational thought. "I think that would be for the best."

"As do I," Stephen replied, and then he bent down and claimed her lips again.

Epilogue

Stephen Frederick Wright, Viscount Endicott, took a sip of champagne from a crystal flute and then smiled as he heard the sound of Diana's laughter. His eyes searched the throng that crowded into the ballroom until he spotted her dark head among a clump of well-wishers standing near the entranceway. He, himself, had spent the last hour accepting the congratulations from friends and acquaintances who viewed this wedding as simply the long-expected conclusion to their four-month engagement that had lasted nearly all the season.

Only Diana's family and his closest friends knew the truth, that this wedding had been hastily arranged in the three weeks since Diana had proposed to him. Calling on him in the early hours of the morning, invading his house just as she had invaded every other facet of his life. It was only fitting, he supposed, that she had been the one to propose marriage. Left to his own devices, it might have taken him another few weeks to screw up his courage. Weeks that would have been wasted, while now he could have Diana by his side. As his wife.

The wedding itself had gone off without a hitch. His

brother, George, had sent a note with his congratulations and then given them the best gift of all by staying away on the appointed day. The rift between the two brothers would be slow to heal, but there was hope.

And now he had Diana, and his life, which had been set in a predictable course, was now filled with endless possibilities. It was exhilarating, as was the thought that soon his frustration would be at an end, and he could teach Diana the joy of lovemaking.

"You are looking rather tense for a man who has just received everything he ever wanted," Tony Dunne said, coming to stand next to him.

"I was wondering how long I had to wait before I threw this lot out into the streets and had Diana to myself," Stephen replied.

Tony grinned at him. "If you recall, when Elizabeth and I were married, we made our escape after the first hour of the reception. I advise you to do the same. There'll be no getting rid of this crowd, not as long as the servants keep pouring champagne and your chef keeps supplying delicacies."

Stephen nodded. "A good plan. We have to be on our way soon enough. The carriage will take us to Dover, and from there we will board a ship."

"You are taking Diana to Italy?"

"Yes," Stephen said. "Venice to start, and then Florence and Rome. If the climate suits us, we may winter there and return in the spring."

"Or we may go to Greece and then on to Egypt," Diana said, linking her arm in his. "If I can convince Stephen to extend our trip."

"We are not exploring the Nile," Stephen said. "We

are not going looking for crocodiles. I will not take you camel trekking to see the Pyramids."

Her eyes sparkled. "See? He is already weakening," she said to Tony Dunne.

Stephen bit his lips, repressing a smile.

"I will make an adventurer of you yet," Diana told him.

"I think you already have," Stephen replied.